DREAM CALLER

A DREAM SEEKER NOVEL

MICHELLE SHARP

*Keep Dreaming —
Michelle Sharp*

Copyright © 2015 Michelle Sharp

ISBN No. 978-0-9967395-3-5

All rights reserved under International and Pan-American Copyright Conventions

By payment of required fees, you have been granted the *non*-exclusive, *non*-transferable right to access and read the text of this book. No part of this text may be reproduced, transmitted, downloaded, decompiled, reverse engineered, or stored in or introduced into any information storage and retrieval system, in any form or by any means, whether electronic or mechanical, now known or hereinafter invented without the express written permission of copyright owner.

Please Note

The reverse engineering, uploading, and/or distributing of this book via the internet or via any other means without the permission of the copyright owner is illegal and punishable by law. Please purchase only authorized electronic editions, and do not participate in or encourage electronic piracy of copyrighted materials. Your support of the author's rights is appreciated.

No part of this book may be reproduced or transmitted in any form or by any electronic or mechanical means, including photocopying, recording or by any information storage and retrieval system, without the written permission of the publisher, except where permitted by law.

Cover Design and Interior format by The Killion Group
http://thekilliongroupinc.com

Thank you.

DEDICATION:

To P.B.

Thank you for picking up so much of the slack. Everything I accomplish is only possible because of your support. Love you always. -H.B.

ACKNOWLEDGEMENTS:

I'm always humbled by the many wonderful and supportive people around me who allow me to pursue this crazy dream of writing. To my husband, family, and mom, thank you for your love and support. And thank you for not caring that the house is a bit messier while I write. Also, thank you for seeing the fact that I cook less and less as a good thing.

Thank you to my BFF, Cindy. Your friendship means everything.

To the cosmos girls: Claudia, Linda, Tammy, and Dana, once again a big thank you for all the time and hard work you put into the critiques. Our little group brings much happiness into my life.

Thank you to my very gifted editor, Beth Hill. You make my writing better in a million different ways.

Thank you to the Killion Group for the wonderful work they do. Kim, thank you for a beautiful cover. Jen, thank you for being patient and amazing with the million things I ask of you. And Jenn, thank you for proofreading so thoroughly. You are the queen of commas and repetitive words.

Most of all thank you to the readers who keep inviting Ty and Jordan back into your life. I'm forever grateful.
Never stop dreaming,
Michelle

PROLOGUE

"It's so freaking cold," she murmurs, stomping through the icy street. She looks ahead at the lit sidewalk along the road, then contemplates the snow-blanketed field to her left. "Screw it. I'm taking the short cut."

Her white parka and boots blend with the frozen ground as though she's a disembodied pair of Levis tromping through the slush-filled ravine. The crunch-crunch of her steps is the only sound in the frigid night.

She stops, looks behind, then ahead. "Shouldn't have come this way, it's so damn creepy." She moves on, then stops. Moves. Stops. An eerie game to see if the echoing footsteps quiet the same moment hers do.

"Who's there?" Picking up the pace, she turns and walks faster, but so does the echo.

She starts to run.

"Hailey."

When she stops and sees him, her breath shudders out with relief. "Holy crap, David. You scared the hell out of me. I almost peed myself." Retreating back to where he stands, she puts her arms around his waist and kisses his neck. "I'm sorry we fought."

She stares up at him, but her apology is met with silence. "You're still mad?"

His silence continues.

"I'm sorry, David. I didn't want to do it there. I mean, a frat party? I love you, but can't we do better for our first time?"

"Our first time? Doesn't that figure?" He steps closer and shakes his head. "You have no idea, Hailey. I'm going to do so much better." Gently, he brushes a finger down her cheek.

"You're still drunk. Your eyes look really weird," she teases. "I see you found your coat and hat." She crinkles her nose. "Yuck. You need to wash it. It smells like that smoky, stinky frat house."

He glances around. "I thought you'd stay on the street, take the long way home."

"I know you worry, but it was so late, and I was tired and cold. After our fight, I just wanted to go home. Walk me the rest of the way?"

He nods, but as she turns to walk on, he fists his hand into her hair and yanks her back.

"Ow. What the hell?"

He spins her around. His fist connects with her cheek, then her jaw, and she drops to her knees.

"David?"

"You should be mine," he screams, then he lowers his voice as if realizing his mistake. "All of this, every fucking thing here should be mine. You're just one more blonde reminder of how unfair this fucking world is."

"I am yours. What are you talking about? We've been together every day since school started. How could you doubt the way I feel about you?"

"I don't doubt it, Hailey. And it's exactly the reason you've got to die."

CHAPTER 1

When attempting a normal relationship, it was vital to appear normal. Jordan Delany reminded herself of the new mantra she'd adopted the day she'd said yes to moving in with Tyler McGee.

But as she lay on the wooden floor of their new bedroom, unable to move and shivering from the latest dream, three things became abundantly clear. First, the ceiling could use a fresh coat of paint. Second, she didn't have a snowball's chance in hell at pulling off normal. And last, it sucked to be thirty. Scraping herself off the floor wasn't coming nearly as easily as it had at twenty.

Forty was going to be a bitch.

As a St. Louis narcotics detective, she often crossed paths with drugs, violence, and murder. In addition, she had the handy-dandy ability to connect with spirits of dead victims through her dreams. So she had no grand illusions of ever making it to fifty. At least there was that.

Her legs needed more time to steady before she stood. This she knew from years of experience. Her skin was damp with sweat, and the cold air in the room made her shudder. Recognizing the trembling as her system's attempt to warm itself after she witnessed a young woman die in the snow, she went with it, let the sensations swallow her. Fighting the tremors only prolonged the time her body needed to recover from a dream.

She closed her eyes and let the details of the latest vision solidify.

This dream had been different from most. Usually the victim was the focus.

Their fear.

Their adrenaline.

Their struggle for life.

And yes, she had felt all that. She'd seen the girl's long blonde hair and petite build.

But the odd thing was how clearly she'd seen the attacker. Usually a faceless shadow was the best she had to work with. Not this time. His shaggy, curly blond hair was as crystal clear as his pretty hazel eyes. He was tall and lean, with the athletic build of a swimmer.

The girl had known her attacker. Trusted him, even. Walked to him and wrapped her arms around him. Maybe that was why she could see him so vividly. The young woman had been in love with the young man who killed her.

Hard to be *that* wrong about someone.

She thought about her own romantic relationship. Ty had asked her to move in with him. How long would it be before he'd admit to being wrong? Quite simply, although he knew more about her than anyone else ever had, he hadn't lived with her long enough to understand the insanity that went along with her visions.

He knew she dreamed. He knew the dreams often contained visions or messages about a case she was involved with. And he knew her darkest secret—those messages came from the dead.

Surprisingly, he loved her, anyway.

So she worked out a doable standoff with death. During the day she blocked all spirits. In turn, they came any damn time they pleased at night in her dreams.

Granted, not a perfect solution, especially with her attempting a relationship for the first time. But the mutual understanding between her and the dead worked.

She no longer feared Ty leaving because of the violent nightmares she endured. Although every dream he *didn't* witness was a point in her "normal" column.

This morning, Ty had been called away on a murder investigation. She hadn't been happy that their much-needed vacation had been cut short, but there was an upside. The murder had kept him from witnessing another doozy of a dream. Yet if he *were* there, he'd have lifted her off the floor and taken her back to bed. The thought of what he might have done after that sent a small spear of warmth through her shaking body

Something shifted beside Jordan. Startled, she gasped. The gasp had been neither cop-like nor Jordan-like, a clear sign she hadn't recovered from the images in the dream. The shifting hairball whined and inched closer.

"I'm okay, Beauty."

Having a pet was as new to Jordan as was living with a man. In less than a week she'd gone from a lifetime of being solo to having two roommates. She slung an arm around Beauty, a yellow Lab stray that had collapsed on their property after a run-in with a coyote.

One of Beauty's ears looked like it had been through a shredder. Half of her body was shaved in a willy-nilly pattern that resembled random crop circles. Yet despite being esthetically challenged, the dog had a kind spirit and soulful eyes that rivaled Ty's. Particularly when it came to wrapping around Jordan's heart. A fact she didn't intend to admit to either one of them.

"All right, let's get up, girl."

Beauty stood in a flash despite having twenty-four stitches in assorted spots on her body. Jordan didn't move nearly as fast.

"I don't suppose I could train you to fetch me a blanket and my journal?"

Beauty tilted her head, looking puzzled.

"Didn't think so. But you probably need to potty, huh?"

Now Beauty gave her the *duh* eyes.

"Okay, we'll pee and get coffee. Can you operate a Keurig?"

The dog wagged her tail with confidence.

"Good, let's go. Momma needs a little caffeine."

Hopefully, there would be time to journal the dream before she was called into work because a vision like the one she'd just had could only mean one thing.

A new case was on the horizon.

Tyler McGee pulled to a stop on Blueberry Street, more commonly referred to as "fraternity row." He grabbed gloves and a couple of essentials from his truck and moved in the direction of the crime scene tape.

An hour before, he'd been wrapped around Jordan, another week of vacation stretching out before him. Now he was freezing his ass off in a late winter snow, about to take a look at a dead body.

The officer stationed outside the tape was one he knew well. His brother's best friend, Caleb Jones.

"Hey, Jonesy. How you doing?"

"Better than our victim, that's for sure," Jones returned.

"Bad one?" Ty asked. "Let's have it."

"We have an ID from two sorority sisters. Victim is Hailey King, nineteen-year-old female student in Lincoln University's nursing program. Her roommates got worried when she didn't return last night. Said it wasn't like her. So early this morning they decided to backtrack to the frat house where they all partied last night. There's a ravine right over there." Jones pointed behind the sorority house. "Rather than walk around the block, the kids use it as a cut-through between houses. They found the victim in the center of the ravine."

Ty looked over to where Jones pointed. "They touch the body?"

"Big time. Said they thought maybe she had too much to drink and passed out or something. Sounds like they didn't even let the fact that she could be dead enter their minds. She was face down, so they shook her and then turned her over. When they saw her bloody face, they realized it was too late. You would think two nursing students would know better than to touch all over a victim like that, but I guess they didn't."

Spoken like a man who'd never happened upon the dead body of someone he cared about.

"Composure and common sense mean nothing when you're in denial. Training and rules..." Ty shook his head. "... mean nothing if your heart thinks you can bring them back, even if deep down you know differently."

Jonesy visibly cringed, and Ty was pretty sure the bell had finally gone off in his head. Ty had stood over his sister's dead body, and he wouldn't have given two shits about procedure or logic if he thought he could have brought Tara back.

"Sorry, man. I didn't mean to say something stupid."

Ty worked up a smile. Jonesy was a good cop and knew all too well what had happened to Tara. "You didn't say anything stupid. Just cop-like. I better get to it." Ty pulled on his rubber gloves.

"Uh, you might want to hold up a minute." A big grin spread across Jonesy's face. "You know that saying about a woman being a *brick*"— he did a mild hip thrust—"*house?*"

Ty narrowed his eyes.

"Let it filter through your mind as you turn around." Jonesy slapped a hand against Ty's shoulder. "Then enjoy the view. You got company, dude."

Ty squeezed his eyes shut. *Hell no* was his first thought.

He did an about-face and watched the saucy little redhead from Missouri Highway Patrol arrow straight for him. His second thought: *If there is a gracious God in this world, please don't allow this woman and Jordan to ever, ever cross paths.*

"Why, Tyler McGee." The new arrival met his gaze with equal parts humor, confidence, and—he was pretty sure—revenge woven into her sultry smile. "Fate has brought us together again."

Be professional. Act like nothing happened. Ty nodded, pulled off the glove, and offered a handshake. "Isobel, nice to see you."

"So you do remember my name? I thought maybe you couldn't look me up because your memory was bad." She glared at his outstretched hand. "Surely you can do better than a handshake, McGee."

"Oh, well, I, uh . . ." *Nope. Not going to be okay.* What the fuck was he supposed to say? "So I guess you got an early call today, too? You made it in record time."

"Your chief called mine, said there was a murder. I was told you were on vacation." She shrugged. "I was closest, so I came. No big deal. You guys always need us for all the lab work, anyway."

"Listen, Isobel, if this is going to be a problem—"

"Relax, McGee." She laughed. "You're not the first or the last guy I've slept with who's forgotten how to use the phone the next day. I knew the score going in: likely to be one night only. It's fine."

He relaxed a little; she didn't appear to be out for blood. Nobody ever accused him of being a saint, but no female could ever accuse him of being less than respectful. Or of casually mixing business with pleasure. *Except* for Isobel Riley. She'd caught him on a particularly bad night on both counts. "I'm sorry if

I hurt your feelings. I had a lot to drink after a grueling case. I probably wasn't thinking clearly."

"I worked that case, too, Ty. I remember it well."

She gave him a smile that he just *knew* was going to cause trouble with Jordan.

"We should probably get to work." She headed toward the crime scene and then turned back. "Although you did get the sex, so I think the least you could do is buy me a meal when we're done here."

Yep. Fucking trouble with a capitol T.

CHAPTER 2

Jordan picked up a note from the kitchen counter.
Don't forget dinner at my parents' house tonight. Love you. Ty.

She frowned. Like she didn't have enough anxiety just trying to figure out how to be in a relationship. Why did she have to meet the parents? At least he hadn't invited them to the ranch; thank God she didn't have to fake her way through cooking a meal. Not that she could actually find the stove under all the crap.

She and Ty had moved into a big old estate and horse ranch with the intention of restoring it. Apparently, Ty had thought about purchasing the vacant property for years. Knowing his determination to once again see the house and stables vibrant and alive, she believed the end result would be spectacular. Right now, the place was a disaster.

The cluster of odds-and-ends junk was driving her mad. She eyeballed Ty's trash on the countertop. "Breakfast of champions," she murmured, picking up the empty milk carton and throwing away his Heath candy wrapper. Ty's dream was to own horses, but the man needed a damn dairy farm the way he went through milk.

She didn't consider herself compulsive about cleanliness, but she'd never had to live with anyone else's candy wrappers and milk cartons piling up, either. Not to mention the staggering number of tools the man left everywhere. In one fell swoop, she shoved all the tools and junk into an empty drawer and wiped down the countertops and table.

Friend and co-worker FBI Special Agent Ted Bahan was on his way over to check out their new home. At least that was the excuse he gave for the impromptu visit. After this morning's dream,

Jordan knew it was very possible her vacation was about to get cut as short as Ty's. She'd lay money on Bahan having a new case for her.

Either that or he had information about her dad.

A week ago, one of Bahan's FBI buddies made an offhand remark about working with a Special Agent named Jack Delany. Jack Delany had been Jordan's father's name, and Jordan was still attempting to blow off the remark as nothing more than a coincidence.

Beauty must have heard Bahan's car, because she began barking. It was the first time Jordan had heard the sound. More of a lazy *roo-roo-roo* than a bark, but she decided it counted all the same.

"Hey, you do have a voice. I was beginning to think that mean old coyote had chewed out your barker." Jordan patted the dog's head and made her way to the front of the house.

Bahan was walking up the porch steps when she opened the door.

Beauty stepped out in front of her.

Bahan stopped abruptly. "What is that?" He flashed an amused smile. Most days, his normal blond-haired, blue-eyed GQ-ness made lesser FBI agents appear downright frumpy. Today's dress code was a rare event. He wore jeans in lieu of one of his expensive suits.

"What do you mean? It's my dog, Beauty." Jordan fought off a smile. Beauty's name was more ironic than accurate. And would likely remain so until her hair grew back.

"What happened to it?"

"She ran into a coyote out in the woods behind the house. The vet had to shave her so he could stitch her up."

"The man was no artist with a razor, was he?" Bahan chuckled and scratched Beauty's head. "Why does it not surprise me that *your* dog would go off half-cocked and pick a fight she couldn't possibly win?" He shook his head. "The FBI gives classes on how to properly evaluate a threatening situation. Maybe you and your dog could both benefit from the course."

Jordan snickered. "Shut up, dickhead." Still, she couldn't deny that a couple of months ago her face would have made Beauty appear downright pretty in comparison. A three-hundred-pound drug dealer had beaten the hell out of her and left her to die in a deserted field. Ty had saved her life, but she had to admit that she and Beauty both looked like they'd been knocked around with the same ugly stick.

Bahan followed her inside. "Where's McGee? I thought he'd be here. I brought him a case of beer as a house-warming."

"He was planning on it, but he got called in on a case this morning. A murder. Which almost never happens around here, so it was a pretty big deal."

She gave him the tour of the house, let him poke around, and then led him into the kitchen.

He walked to the back window. "Man, when you go all domestic, you do it right—house, dog, a big chunk of land. This place is huge."

"I know, right? Who'd have guessed?"

"And look at the size of that barn."

"Don't let Ty hear you call it that. It's a stable, not a barn. Meant to house race horses, not keep chickens and tractors. Apparently, there's a difference."

She fired up the coffee maker and Bahan leaned a hip on the counter and smiled at her. "You look good. Like you're really happy."

She paused and thought about Bahan's observation. She did feel more alive, more like a normal person—with real hope of having a normal life—than she ever had before. "I really am happy, I think." She turned away from Bahan's assessing stare, embarrassed by how huge those words felt.

"Are you blushing? Jordan Delany, warrior cop of the drug world?" he teased. "Holy crap, McGee's made you soft. You're like a schoolgirl with a crush."

She grabbed a kitchen towel and snapped it at him. "I'm a schoolgirl who will kick your ass."

He dodged her attack. "Yee-haw, bad-ass Jordan Delany is now a ranch mama. You'll probably be pregnant and barefoot the next time I visit."

She flipped him off and turned to grab the coffee mugs.

"I'm just joking around." His voice was softer now, more sincere. "I'm happy for you. Everybody deserves a little domestic happiness, I guess."

She shot him a sideways glance. "Yeah. What about you?"

"Everybody who wants it, that is," he said, quickly backtracking. "I know nothing about domestic happiness. The only family time I ever enjoyed was when my old man passed out before he stumbled his way home. I'll take bad guys and bullets any day over this domestic crap." He stared down at Beauty. "No offense."

They went to the table and sat. "Well, don't tell Ty, but sometimes all this domestic crap scares the hell out of me, too. But if I'm ever going to give it a shot, I think now's the time. And I think now might also be a good time to pull back on some of the long-term undercover. Don't get me wrong, I still want to do the job. It's just—"

Bahan held up his hand. "I get it. It's a hard life. Especially when you're starting a relationship. Technically I'm not your boss, though. I only put the task forces together. You're going to have to run this by your commander."

"I've already mentioned it to him."

Bahan shook his head. "Jordan Delany in love. I never thought I'd see the day. You are *really* screwed."

She smiled over the top of her mug. "Seems that way, doesn't it."

Bahan reached into his computer bag and pulled out a file folder. He slid it toward her. "I was hoping McGee would be here when I gave this to you."

Neither of them spoke. The innocent manila folder sent Jordan's heartbeat into a wild, racing rhythm. A file folder wasn't how Bahan typically got her up to speed on a new case. She turned it enough to see the label. *Jack Delany*.

Her stomach churned as if the coffee had been tainted with spoiled milk. "So it's true?" she murmured.

He nodded. "It's true."

"My dad was FBI?"

"For about seven years," he confirmed. "He was a St. Louis city cop before that."

She swallowed, choking down a lifetime of believing her dad had been a drug dealer. "So I've hated my dad for twenty years, called him every name in the book because I thought he was dealing drugs. But in reality he was doing the same job I do?"

"I've only had the file since yesterday, so I haven't had time to comb through every detail yet. It looks like he was in deep cover with a cartel when things went south for him and another agent. The case file has been sealed for twenty years. It only became available a month or so ago. It's all on this disk." He held up the plastic case. "But I'd like to keep the disk."

Puzzled, she looked at him. "Why would you keep it?"

"I could put together a better picture for you if you give me some time. Some of the information I've printed for you to see, some I haven't. If I keep the disk, you could ask questions any time you need answers. I can help you—"

She pushed back from the table. "I don't need you to go through the file for me. Do you think I need a damn keeper?" She stood and stomped over to the sink, then slammed down her coffee mug.

"I didn't say you needed a keeper." He followed her. "There are reasons cops aren't allowed to investigate cases related to them. Realistically, if it were my family, there might be things I wouldn't care to know or see."

"That's bullshit. You'd want to know every last detail, just like I do. I mean seriously, I already tried and convicted my dad. Spent twenty years convinced he was nothing more than a drug-dealing loser only to find out he was a cop. Is there really anything else that could make me feel like a bigger shit right now?"

"Believe it or not, I think so." He paused until she made eye contact. "There are crime scene photos on the disk."

She shrugged. "So?"

"So?" he repeated. "Are you fucking kidding me?"

"You think I haven't seen crime scene photos? How long have you known me?"

"I think you haven't seen them of your own family's murder."

"I was there, Bahan." She slammed a hand down on the old ceramic countertop. "What part do you think I don't remember? The gunshots? Hiding in the closet with the smell of vomit and piss all over me? Crawling through my dad's blood to try to shake him awake? And you're going to stand there and tell me I can't take whatever is on that disk?"

Bahan went still for a moment, then rubbed at the back of his neck. "I'm not saying you can't take it. I'm saying you don't have to take it, at least not alone."

She closed her eyes and took a breath, reminded herself he was trying to help, trying to be a good friend. He didn't deserve her wrath. "I'm sorry. I know you're trying to protect me from an ugly truth." She laid her hand on top of his. "It's way too late for that. I need to know what really happened that night."

"Do you? Do you need to know every little detail? Because it seems like you're happy now. What if that folder takes you back to a place that you've spent a lot of years trying to get away from? Digging up the past could make everything worse."

She thought about the reoccurring nightmares, about all the questions, about the twisted resentment for her father that had been based on a lie. "It could also make everything better. I think I need to take that chance."

He studied her face, her posture. She made no other pleas. Finally, he nodded. "Okay. Since McGee's not here, I'll stay. We can go through it together."

"So what do you think?" Ty asked Isobel as they stared down at the lifeless body of the young blonde nursing student.

"Well, whoever it was did a number on her. Her face is covered in blood. But ultimately, I think cause of death was strangulation." Isobel bent down and looked closer at the victim's neck. "Could be a head trauma we can't see, but I doubt it."

"I agree. Someone was angry and gave her a few good blows to the face, but I'd also wager that whatever caused those marks on her neck is what killed her." Ty gently turned one of her hands over. "She wasn't wearing gloves. Hopefully she's got enough DNA under her nails to fry someone."

"All right." Isobel stood. "Pictures are done. Diagrams are done. I'll tell the coroner he can have her if you're okay with it."

Jonesy approached with an evidence bag in his hand. "If she had any cash, it's gone, but her iPhone and iPad weren't touched."

"Yeah," Ty said, "this wasn't a mugging gone wrong. Even if she dropped the purse somewhere back there and he didn't see it, a thief would've taken those diamond earrings. If they're real, you could pawn them for a good chunk of change."

"You ready to talk to her roommates?" Isobel asked.

"Lead the way, Detective Riley," Ty answered.

She waited until they were out of earshot of the other cops. "You can still call me Issy. Detective Riley is a bit formal, considering."

"I was trying to keep it professional."

"That's your loss," she said with a flirty smile.

"Isobel." He stopped walking and waited for her to turn around. "There's something I should make clear. I'm seeing someone."

"Seeing someone the way you saw me that night? Or is there more?"

"A lot more," he said. "We're living together."

"I guess that's your loss, too," she said and winked at him. "That doesn't mean you don't still owe me a meal."

"Fair enough," he said with a great deal of relief. Isobel had taken the news well, and he felt better for being upfront. Still, no need to shoot himself in the foot. The less Jordan knew about Isobel Riley, the better.

"The thing about losing someone when they're young is that they never age in your mind. I don't have any memories of him ever being in a uniform. Mom told us he was a salesman." Jordan ran a fingertip over the picture of her father in his dress blues. "I wonder what he'd look like today, twenty years later? And what my mom and Katy would look like?"

Bahan was quiet until she glanced up. "Sorry." She gestured to the documents. "Guess I got caught up for a second."

"I've opened a Pandora's box for you, and McGee's going to kick my ass when he finds out I did it when he wasn't here."

Jordan grinned and just to piss him off, clucked like a chicken. "Are you scared of Ty, Bahan?" she teased. "I had no idea."

"I am *not* scared of him, but I don't need your big ape of a boyfriend hacked off at me. I can't very well shoot him, not without a crapload of paperwork."

Jordan laughed. "He may be big, but he's harmless."

"To *you,* maybe. He's obsessed with *you,* thinks *you* walk on water. I'm just the asshole that brought the folder that threw you into a tailspin."

Insulted, she narrowed her eyes at him. "Thank you for your confidence in my mental stability."

"I just think stepping back in time may not be as easy as you think."

"I know." She wanted to argue, say that she'd make it through this just fine. Yet truthfully, her stomach was already in knots. "You're right. I've thought about little else since Bellows walked into my office last week and asked if my father could have been FBI. I've played the *what if* game a hundred or more times."

She shrugged and picked up the picture of her father again. "It makes such perfect sense, you know. My dad was never a bad guy. Never abusive or mean. He loved us, I know he did. It pisses me off that I'm trained to look beyond the obvious lies on the surface, yet I was too messed up to dig deeper for my own dad. Part of me wants to hate myself for it, but I also know there's a reason I blamed him. I mean, I asked questions. Even at ten years old, I had good bullshit radar. For some reason, everyone around me hid the truth. Now I need to know why."

"Maybe *why* isn't as important as knowing that your old man was a good guy. Couldn't that be enough?"

She looked up at Bahan. This time she wanted—no, she *needed*—the truth. The real truth. "No, it isn't enough. There was a very specific reason I was led to believe my dad was a drug dealer. I can't take back all the years I hated him, but I can do this much for him."

She flipped through a few more documents. "Who is this?"

Bahan took a mugshot from her hand. "He was the shooter."

"No." She took the photo back, studied it closer. "No, this isn't him."

"His name was Anton Linder. The reports state that the first responding officers caught this guy"—Bahan tapped the picture in her hand—"fleeing from your house. And there's something else you should know. Linder had connections to a very powerful cartel. Care to take a guess as to which?"

No way. Jordan's gaze locked on to Bahan's. "Delago?"

"Bingo."

Memories of her last case surfaced quickly, memories of being beaten nearly to death by a drug distributor for the Delago cartel. The low-grade churning in her gut kicked up another notch. "Jesus. Fate certainly has a way of fucking with you, doesn't it?" She took a few deep breaths, determined to stay focused in front of Bahan.

"I knew the Delago family was powerful and has been around for years, but . . ."

"But nothing. This is why I'd prefer you let me check into things before you go poking around. It's going to take hours and hours to look through all the documents on that disk and piece everything together." Bahan scrubbed his hands up and down his face. "I knew I shouldn't have brought this to you today. Just *knew* I'd never be able to talk any sense into you."

"I'm fine." Bahan had a lot of power and connections; she couldn't afford to lose his support now. "Look, I'm not stupid enough to think I can remain completely emotionless; it *was* my family. But I've got a handle on it and I won't let my feelings interfere. I'll treat this like any other case—gather facts and figure out what really happened. And whatever the truth turns out to be, I'm not going to let it affect my life right now."

He studied her for a long moment, as if he didn't believe anything she'd just said.

Finally, she pleaded her case one more time. "Believe it or not, the truth doesn't make things harder. Knowing my dad was FBI, knowing he was doing the right thing . . . it helps. Someone murdered my family. That's not ever going to change. But knowing who pulled the trigger, and understanding why . . . I think that'll help, too."

He nodded. "I want that closure for you, but only on one condition. If I say you're done, you're done."

"Bossy, much?" Jordan smiled her agreement. Then she picked up the picture of the man identified as the shooter. "Let's start here." She shook her head. "This is not who shot my family."

"According to the report, he is." Bahan flipped through the stack of papers, pulled out a document, started giving Jordan a rundown. "The first cops to arrive saw that man, identified as Anton Linder, thirty-two, of St. Louis, run from your house, jump into a 1982 Ford Mercury, and flee the scene."

Bahan handed her the report. "There were two cops. One got out of the cruiser and went into your house. The other followed the suspect a few miles until Linder crashed, killing himself. The gun used in the shootings was in the car with Linder. Ballistics matched. He had the murder weapon right next to him. His fingerprints were all over it."

"I can't help what the report says—something isn't right." With absolute certainty she knew Linder was *not* the man she had seen over and over in her dreams. "The man I saw was tall and thin, had long black hair, Native American features, and a big red scar that ran from his eye down to the bottom of his cheek. Time may dull a lot, but it's never dulled what that son of a bitch looks like. I'd know him anywhere."

Bahan leaned back in the chair and sighed. "I thought you said you didn't actually see the shooter? That you were hiding in a closet while your mom, dad, and sister were killed?"

That was true. Technically, she didn't see the shots fired on the night of the murders. But she'd seen the shooter very clearly in her dream. Every feature, every scar, every strand of hair, every cadence of his body. "I had a dream the night before the murders. That's when I saw him."

"You believe this"—Bahan held up the mugshot—"was *not* the guy who killed your family based on a dream you had over twenty years ago? You said you were going to try to be objective. Two different policemen stated that this guy ran from your house and jumped into a car. The bullets that killed your family match the gun they found sitting next to this guy. He was a local dealer working for the Delago family, notorious for being one of their lynch men. What conclusion would you draw from that?"

"It sounds like a slam dunk, I know. But no one besides me was there. They weren't inside the house. They didn't see."

"Neither did you," he accused. "You were hiding."

This—the disbelief from others—was always going to accompany her gift. "How did I know the drug transfer was going to happen in Titus on our last case?"

He paused, conceding the point. "A dream. I get that." Then he tilted his head back and shut his eyes briefly, as if channeling patience from some divine power. "I understand about your dreams, and I know how strongly you believe in them, but this is different."

"Why? I was able to give you every last detail we needed to bust our last case wide open."

Bahan said nothing.

"I wasn't wrong then, and I don't think I'm wrong now. Maybe there was more than one shooter. Maybe the guy I saw was there too and freaked when he heard sirens. He could have dropped the gun, and maybe the other guy grabbed it. I don't know for sure, but I think these questions are worth asking."

She fished through a few more documents. Found one from Saunders Funeral Home and Crematorium, which on the surface made sense.

Next she picked up a newspaper article about her family's murder. It wove a bogus tale of a robbery gone wrong. So much for journalistic truth. She brought the picture next to the article closer to get a better look.

She recognized the man in the picture. Her dad's brother Bill. Bill had refused to take her in after the murders, which was why *she* refused to acknowledge his existence to this day. He'd turned his back on her. The way she saw it, he hadn't earned the right to be called uncle. Not then, and not now.

Even so, there was something other than her disdain for Bill that bugged her about the picture. "There shouldn't be caskets if you cremate someone, right?"

Bahan shrugged. He was heavily engrossed in a different document. "I guess not. Probably depends on what the family wants. Why?"

"Because as fucked up as I was when all this was going on, I remember spreading my family's ashes. Bill and I spread them in the lake my family loved to boat on. We didn't have any other family. So what's the deal with this funeral and the caskets? And listen to this, the article reads: *Robbery gone wrong in North St. Louis. Suspect dead.*

"It wasn't a robbery, it was a goddamned ambush. But this doesn't say anything about the drug connection at all. Just that two adults and two children were murdered. But that's not right. Only one child was killed. This doesn't make any sense."

Bahan's knee was bobbing fast enough to shake all the papers on the table, he was so deeply in the zone. "I've got a bad feeling it makes perfect sense. I keep searching for a mention of you—what happened to you after the shooting, what was your statement—but there isn't one. No mention of you surviving anywhere."

Tossing down the document in his hand, Bahan pushed back from the table. "Let me ask you something. If you and I are brought in to clean up after something like this, what do we do with a traumatized little girl who may or may not have witnessed the violent murders of her family? How do we keep her safe from a drug cartel that's going to want all loose ends dealt with?"

Jordan knew where he was going with his questions. "We make her disappear." Jordan propped her elbows on the table, let her head rest in her hands, while her mind toyed with the idea that she'd been unwittingly put into some kind of witness protection program.

"They tried to change my name," she finally murmured. The memory was vague, as most were from the year following her family's death. Probably because they'd poked every anti-depressant and sleeping pill known to man down her throat. "They told me when you live with a foster family that you have to take the family name, but I never would."

Bahan looked at her.

"My name was the only thing I had. I couldn't give that up, too. Plus I have a birth certificate and a social security card. I think all the info is right."

"Are they the same documents you've had since birth? Is the social security number you have now the same one you were born with? Or did it change about the time you were eleven?"

"I don't know. How would I know that? I didn't have my social security number memorized when I was ten."

"Most ten-year-olds don't." Bahan sighed. "It looks to me like the authorities—probably the Feds your dad worked with—made a decision to let the world think you died that night, too. The shooter was dead. He wasn't telling anyone he fucked up and only took out three people instead of four. It was a brilliant way to protect you, when you think about it."

"So that's why I went into foster care in Kansas City instead of St. Louis. They moved me to a different city, altered my documents, and bam, I'm a different Jordan Delany."

"You'd have probably had a different name, too, if you hadn't been such a little shit about it. It's the best theory we've got."

"So the funeral here was just for show? They buried four empty caskets just to protect me. That was a lot of trouble and expense to go through."

Bahan went unusually silent. Which was never good. "Yeah," he finally agreed. "Or maybe they actually did bury three people. And maybe the only empty casket was yours."

CHAPTER 3

Ty and Isobel stepped into the foyer of Hailey King's sorority house. Hailey's two roommates were waiting with a police officer in the next room.

"You want to separate them?" Isobel asked.

"Yeah." Ty glanced at the girls through the large archway. "You take the blonde somewhere else; I'll interview the brunette here. Then we can compare notes."

They walked into a large room that looked well-worn from years of parties. The two young women were huddled together on one of the three couches lining the walls.

Ty pulled an ottoman in front of them and sat. "Hi, ladies. I'm Officer Tyler McGee from the Longdale Police Department. This is Detective Isobel Riley from the Missouri Highway Patrol. We're very sorry about your roommate. We'll do everything in our power to catch whoever did this, but we need to ask you some questions."

The girls nodded.

Ty glanced down at his notes. "Ashley, would you go with Detective Riley?" One girl stood and followed Isobel out of the room.

The other girl grabbed more tissues, ready to cry.

"It's Gena, right?"

She nodded again.

"Hi, Gena. I know this is hard. Can you tell me what happened this morning?"

The girl blew her nose and then said, "Ashley and I had the alarm set for six. We were supposed to help out at a healthcare seminar today. It was for extra credit in one of our classes. Hailey was going too."

She sniffled. "We're all nursing students. When we got up, it didn't look like Hailey had ever been home. She left some clothes and books on her bed last night when she left for the party. I didn't think they'd been moved." Gena shrugged, wiped her eyes again. "We figured she had too much to drink and just stayed at the frat house with David. We decided to go search for her so she didn't get in trouble for being a no-show."

"David?"

"David Benson is Hailey's boyfriend. He's a business student. They've been seeing each other for a while now."

"Were they together last night?"

Gena nodded.

Ty noted the boy's name. David Benson would need to be located. "How long?"

"Since we started school last August. They were pretty serious. She was nuts over him."

"Was that normal? For Hailey to not come home?"

Tears rolled down Gena's face. She shook her head. "No, not at all. I mean, she would come home late sometimes, way after Ash and I would be asleep. But she never spent the whole night with David. It's kind of frowned upon. David has a roommate. It's pretty tacky to hook up in a room when another guy is sleeping there. And Hailey was sort of . . . um . . . old-fashioned about those kind of things."

"Old-fashioned meaning what?"

"Meaning she wouldn't sleep around or hook up with random guys walking in and out of a frat room. She was just, sweet, you know? A good girl who got good grades and . . ."

Gena dropped her head in her hands and started sobbing. Ty sat quietly and let her cry. He knew what being on that side of the questions felt like.

"I'm sorry."

"Don't be sorry, Gena. You're doing a fantastic job. Do you need something to drink?"

Gena wiped the tears away with a tissue. "I'm okay."

"Do you have any reason to believe her boyfriend would hurt her?"

"I can't see it. David was always really protective of Hailey. Like I said, they were pretty crazy about each other. He walked her home every night. In fact, I looked out the window last night and saw him leaning against a tree watching the sorority house. I figured he was waiting for Hailey to get inside safely. I told Ashley I saw him, and that's when we turned out the light. I just assumed Hailey was home safe."

"You saw David outside the sorority house? What time was that?"

"I'm not sure exactly. One maybe. No, wait. Probably more one-thirty-ish. I'm not sure."

"Are you positive it was him?"

"It'd be hard to confuse David with anyone else. He's really tall and thin. And he's got all this blond, bushy hair that sticks out from under that Cubs hat he always wears." Gena shrugged. "Not too many guys look like David."

"Did David ever seem overly protective? Jealous? Ever violent?"

"No. See, that's why I don't want to say stuff. He wasn't like that at all. He was really cool about her hanging out with us."

"Gena, you're doing the right thing for Hailey. Everything you're telling me helps me to catch who did this. I'm not looking for an easy person to blame. I'm looking for a killer. If you tell me Hailey's boyfriend was a good guy who was concerned and understanding, that doesn't paint him as someone who would hurt her. But I have to ask the questions, okay?"

"Okay."

"Do you know where David is from? Where he grew up?"

Gena shook her head. "I know he has money. A lot of it. He gave Hailey a diamond necklace last week for their six-month anniversary. She hasn't taken it off since."

She didn't have it on when they'd found her, Ty recalled. "Anyone else you know of who might have a personal grudge against her? Anyone bother her recently? Fight with her?"

The girl sat for a long moment without saying anything. Finally, she stared up at Ty. "She had a big fight with David last night."

Ty stepped outside of Hailey King's sorority house and waited for Isobel on the porch. Big houses with Greek letters lined a good portion of the street. In the distance, majestic old buildings made for a pretty campus as they spread over several city blocks.

His gloomy exhale hung in the cold morning air. It should have been a place where life was beginning, not ending.

He loved his job. Most days. Today wasn't gonna be one of 'em. First he'd need to explain to a young woman's family that their daughter had been murdered. Then shake up another family when he had to question the most logical suspect—Hailey's boyfriend.

On top of it, he was tip-toeing through a sea of eggshells with Isobel, praying hard that the one night they'd had together wasn't going to haunt the hell out of him. Technically, it had been more like ten minutes. Ten lousy minutes filled with a bad attitude, too much beer, and less than stellar sex.

And a whole bunch of remorse the second it was over.

He'd been well aware that Isobel was interested in more than a professional relationship. The problem was, he'd never been interested in having anything with her. He didn't dislike her; she was cute and a pretty good cop. But whatever that spark was, the one you were supposed to feel when you sleep with someone, it had never been there.

Unfortunately, she'd unzipped his pants and rolled a condom on him before he was absolutely sure that he felt absolutely nothing. And that just seemed like piss-poor timing. His beer-hazed brain had reasoned that it might insult her more to stop than to politely part ways after.

In comparison, he remembered catching sight of Jordan for the first time—across a sea of drunks in a dirty, disgusting strip club—and feeling like someone had clamped jumper cables to his heart. Until then, he'd thought love at first sight was a damn dumb thing to believe in.

His stomach gave a queasy jerk. Probably the candy bar he had for breakfast. Or the guilty fear that somehow the ten minutes he spent with Isobel was going to wreak havoc with the lifetime he intended to spend with Jordan.

And his fear would come to fruition unless he could close this case in record time and keep the women from ever coming face to face.

"Done already?" Isobel asked, stepping out onto the porch of the sorority house.

"Been done for a few minutes. What took you so long?"

"I like to be thorough the first time around."

"I was thorough."

"I'll bet you lunch that I got more info than you did."

Ty nodded. "Okay. Shoot."

Isobel proceeded to run down the same information he'd just gotten.

"That's you're thorough investigation? I got that much."

Isobel held up a finger. "Excuse me, I'm not done. Hailey was at a mixer last night. It was Hailey's sorority and her boyfriend's, David Benson's, frat house. Apparently they had a big fight." She shot him a cocky grin.

"You've got nothing lunch worthy." Ty laughed at her superior smile.

"Do you know why they were fighting?" she asked.

Ty folded his arms. Sighed. "No. But I intend to find out as soon as I can get to the boyfriend."

"They fought because Hailey was a virgin. It was the six-month anniversary of their first kiss last night, and Hailey had told David she would sleep with him. Turns out she got cold feet because they were in a crowded frat house. But both of them had plenty to drink."

"You got Ashley to spill all that?"

"It's called being thorough." Isobel's smile was triumphant now. "Not only that, but David got a little hotheaded and stormed away. I guess they had words loud enough that several people heard. Then Ashley heard the story first-hand again when Hailey cried on her shoulder last night. And although Hailey was pissed because David went to the basement of the frat house and played poker with some buddies, basically ignoring her the rest of the night, she still stayed when Ashley and Gena left. I guess hoping to make up with David."

"So we've got a wealthy, angry, drunk boyfriend who was promised sex but then got denied." Ty crammed his hands into his coat pockets. "Okay, I guess that's worthy of lunch. See if you can run down priors for David Benson. Gena said she saw him hanging around outside the sorority house last night right about the time

Hailey was murdered. We need to know why. I'm going to make a few phone calls before we talk to him. I want to know where he's from and where he went to high school. And if he so much as got into a fist fight in high school, I want to know about that, too. We'll play it by ear from there."

"Anything you say, slick." Issy winked, and Ty's stomach did the queasy-jerk one more time.

"Let's head to the frat house and find Benson," he said. "And get this case over with pronto," he added when she was well out of earshot.

Ty followed Isobel's car to David Benson's frat house.

"Benson is squeaky clean as far as I can tell," Isobel said as they compared notes and slowly strolled down the walk to the front door. "But do you know who his dad is?"

Ty glanced at Isobel. "Yeah. Doyle Benson. Real estate developer."

"Fucking rich real estate developer. You better make damn sure you advise Benson of his rights before you question him."

Ty stopped and turned toward her. "I'm not questioning anyone as a suspect yet. I'm only gathering info from witnesses."

Isobel arched a brow. "You keep telling yourself that."

"You want to walk away, not talk to him because his dad has money?" he asked.

"No, I want to make sure anything he says sticks. He could turn out to be more than a witness. It's a gray area, and you know it."

"All I know is that if I didn't talk to the people who were with her last, I wouldn't be doing my job." Ty pounded a fist on the door of the frat house. "Nothing gray about it."

A young guy—bleary-eyed and classically hung over—opened the door. Ty announced himself and Isobel, they flashed their badges, and Ty told the kid he needed to speak with David Benson.

Saturday morning in a frat house looked like someone had put a little C4 inside a keg the night before. But to their credit, guys were cleaning up. Probably so they could do it all over again tonight.

"Derek, is Benson in his room?" the young guy shouted.

"I'm not his fucking keeper—oh." The kid who walked into the room flushed ten shades of red when he saw Ty with his badge.

"Keeper or not, one of you needs to find him. Or I'll start a search inside your house, here, that will probably turn up a whole lot of trouble for every member of Phi Beta Dickheads, or whatever you call yourselves."

Isobel snickered when the two guys scrambled up the stairs. "I remember that about you, your way with words."

"Yeah, well, I've learned these young cocky guys speak only asshole. You'd do well to remember it, too."

One of the frat guys returned. "We think he's still in the basement. Probably asleep. They were playing poker until early this morning. It's through that door."

Ty nodded and then headed down the creaky wooden staircase with Isobel behind him. He flipped every light switch he came across.

"Turn the lights off, fucker, we're trying to sleep."

Ty wasn't sure which one of the young guys spoke. He looked around, counted five hungover bodies splayed out on various pieces of old and nasty furniture. An open bag of marijuana sat in full view.

"Disgusting. It stinks down here," Isobel murmured. "And it's going to take us forever to wake these assholes up and figure out which one is Benson."

"Nope, I don't have that kind of time." Ty decided to give them a wake-up call they would never forget. He pulled his gun from the holster. "Cover the stairs and aim at any asshole who moves. Make the show a good one."

He stepped to the middle of the basement, cleared his throat. "You are all under arrest for possession of a controlled substance. Get up. Now." Most of the idiots began to stir. He raised his voice another notch and proceeded as though he'd uncovered a multi-million-dollar drug ring instead of a few bucks worth of weed. "On your knees. Now. Hands behind your head."

Their big eyes started paying attention in a hurry.

"Which one of you is David Benson?"

They were all quick to point at a tall, skinny, curly-haired guy. Ty moved in front of the blond kid that was still slouched on a couch.

"The rest of you, upstairs with Detective Riley. Wait in the front room and answer her questions politely. If you show any disrespect, I will add resisting arrest and assault of an officer to your drug charges. Do we understand each other? Move. Now."

Four guys shuffled upstairs with Isobel.

Ty turned back to the blond kid. "Are you David Benson?"

"Yeah. But that pot isn't mine. I don't smoke; you can ask any of the guys. Do a blood test if you want."

"David, I'm not here because of the pot." Ty looked the kid over, paying careful attention to his hands and face, checking for signs he'd been in a recent struggle. He saw nothing. "Do you have a girlfriend named Hailey King?"

"Yeah," David answered. "But she doesn't do drugs, either. She hardly ever even has a beer. If you found drugs here, she for sure didn't have anything to do with it."

Ty holstered his gun, grabbed a folding chair and straddled it backwards in front of David. "I'm not here because of drugs, David. I'm sorry to have to tell you this. Hailey King was found murdered early this morning. I need to know when you saw her last."

Ty watched the kid's hungover brain attempt to process the information.

"What? Is this some kind of sick joke? Who the fuck are you? Where's Hailey?" The kid shot to his feet.

Ty stood, too. "Sit down, David."

The kid stared at Ty for a moment, and then tears rolled from his eyes. "Who are you?" David asked again, but this time he was struggling to get the words out. "Where is Hailey? I want to see Hailey."

"I'm Officer Tyler McGee from the Longdale Police Department." Ty pulled out his badge, but the kid never even glanced at it. "I'm investigating a murder. I need for you to tell me the last time you saw Hailey King alive."

David collapsed back on the sofa and dropped his head in his hands. "Jesus, I'm dreaming. Having a fucking nightmare."

Ty pulled out a picture of Hailey that her roommate had given him. "Is this your girlfriend?"

David nodded.

"When did you see her last?"

"Last night. She was here at the party until late. We sort of had a fight, so I played poker most of the night in the basement. She stayed upstairs with the girls. I went up to check on her about one or two. I told her I'd put my shoes on and walk her home, but when I got back downstairs, the guys said she already left."

"When did you see her for the last time? Can you narrow it down to a smaller time frame than an hour?"

"I didn't look at the time. I talked to her in the kitchen. It had to be about one. I told her to chill while I went up to my room and got my shoes."

"Then what happened?" Ty asked.

More tears streaked down David's face. "I got my shoes. It took longer than I thought because I was sick. I puked a couple times before I came back downstairs. One of the guys said she got mad and left."

"Did you follow her?"

"I went outside. Looked down the street, but I didn't see her. God, I was still so sick." David plowed his fingers back through his hair.

"Did you follow Hailey at that point?"

"No, I threw up, I think. I kind of don't remember anything after that." David grabbed his phone. "She's at a workshop this morning. A nursing thing. She probably texted me earlier. But that's why you can't find her. She's in town at some kind of—"

"No, David." Ty said. "She isn't missing. Why don't you come to the police station with me so we can talk this through?"

CHAPTER 4

There were seven whole cars in the parking lot of the tiny Longdale precinct when Jordan pulled in next to Ty's truck. Apparently the quiet little town of Longdale was having a red-letter day of crime.

Bahan had another appointment, so they had wrapped up going through her father's file for the day. The break had suited her just fine because the only thing she could concentrate on was the fact that there had been a funeral for her family. A funeral she'd known nothing about.

The lies had already begun to stack up.

She'd thought her father was a drug dealer, but it turned out that he'd been working with the Feds. She'd believed the Native American man in her dream had killed her family, yet now she knew an FBI file claimed someone else entirely had been responsible. And she damn well remembered spreading her family's ashes, so why had a funeral been splashed all over the media?

If there were graves containing her family's names, she intended to see them before the sun went down.

Not having Ty there this morning had been crappy timing. She wanted his take on all of it. He was a good cop. Underneath the disarming charm and killer smile lay a quick mind and a dogged persistence for truth.

Especially when it came to her.

Before Ty, her past wasn't something she shared. Not ever. But Tyler McGee had pursued answers from her like a bloodhound on scent. He'd be just as determined to help her get answers now. And she wasn't gonna lie—there was something about his unrelenting drive she found just as sexy as his gorgeous gray eyes.

She'd made a couple sandwiches and dropped them into a paper bag in case he couldn't get away. Even if cooking wasn't exactly her thing, she could do sliced turkey and chips with the best of them. As she climbed out of her car, she reconsidered bothering him. He wouldn't have been called in from vacation if something big hadn't come up. But even if he was busy, he'd need to eat.

It was Saturday, so no one was sitting at the reception desk inside the door when she entered. She walked a little farther, poked her head into Ty's office. He wasn't there.

Seriously? The place was the size of a porta-potty. Where the hell was everyone? The door to the interrogation room was closed. Maybe he was in there. She walked back to the reception area and leaned against the empty desk to wait for someone to appear.

"Hey, beautiful," said a deep, sexy voice. It wasn't Ty's, but she recognized it all the same. Caleb Jones, one of the cops Ty worked with, was handsome, sweet, and quite the flirt.

She turned around. "Hi, Caleb."

"Looking for Ty?"

"Well, that was the plan."

"Damn," he said. "Why are all the beautiful women here to see him today?"

Let it go, her brain said. *Just let it go.*

Tyler McGee was built like a Viking—tall, heavily muscled. Strong, thick, and solid everywhere. She refused to speculate about how many women in this sleepy little town knew that intimately. Pondering how many damsels in distress walked into his precinct daily looking for him made her brain want to explode. Denial had treated her pretty good over the years, and she saw no reason to screw with the strategy now.

"I thought I might take him to lunch," she said. "Although I know he caught a case, so he might not have time for me."

"If you were my girl, I would always make time for you." Caleb grinned, then looked up and over her shoulder.

Firm fingers tightened around her waist and pulled her back, flush against a hard male body.

Ty.

She'd know his touch with blinders on. And it didn't hurt that the clean scent of his soap had trained her body to react like one of Pavlov's dogs.

"You flirt with my lady again and I'll lock you in the cell," Ty growled over the top of her head.

Jordan knew he was joking, but she picked up on a good amount of fatigue and impatience in his tone. Caleb must have too, because he slipped away without another word.

She turned in Ty's arms and gave him a quick peck on the cheek. "Hi, handsome."

He glanced around the small waiting area. Apparently satisfied that they were alone, he brought his lips down on top of hers. The urgent stroke of his tongue and the wicked little bite on her bottom lip were not his usual MO for a quick hello kiss. He moved his hands to her head, entwined his fingers in her hair, and for just a moment let the kiss spin out.

The surprising intimacy of his actions shook her composure, and honestly, her common sense, too. Yet she recognized that something had knocked him off balance. Breathless, she pushed back a few inches. "Wow. That was some kiss. Did you have a rough morning?" She smoothed his hair away from his eyes.

"You could say that. We got a college girl beaten and murdered. Left for dead in the middle of a ravine."

Ty's jurisdiction wasn't normally a hotbed for murder.

"That sucks." Jordan blew out a breath, understanding exactly why he'd been knocked off center. Didn't it just figure he'd catch a case involving a young murdered girl? "You okay?"

Playfully he tapped her lips with a finger. "I'm better than I was a few minutes ago, thank you very much."

"I'm serious, Ty. It doesn't make you weak if you need to pass this one to someone else." She laid a hand on his chest. "There's no way you can work this case and not think about Tara."

He was quiet for a long moment. "Actually, it's the other way around. There's no way I can think about Tara and *not* work this case. Do you think any other cop wants to catch this asshole more than me?"

She studied his eyes and knew any further arguing was pointless. That dogged persistence again. It arrowed straight to her heart. "No, I don't," she conceded. "And I have no doubt you'll catch the guy. Just don't let it drag you under in the process. Is there anything I can do?"

"Yeah, be ready to leave for my parents when I get home tonight. I've got at least twenty college kids coming in to interview, so I'll probably be running late."

"We could cancel. I'm sure they'll understand that you caught a case. I could make dinner, massage your back. It would be a nice, quiet—"

"Nice try. You must be really desperate to get out of this if you're offering to cook." He tugged her ponytail. "But my parents are chomping at the bit to meet you, and you've succeeded in avoiding them since they got back from Florida. But don't worry. I'll make sure we get home in time for that massage." He winked.

The phone rang on the empty reception desk. "Damn it," he said.

"I won't keep you." He didn't have time for anything else to be put on his plate right now, so she didn't mention her father's case. Instead, she held up the paper bag of sandwiches. "I just wanted to make sure you had something to eat."

"Hang on one second." He reached for the ringing phone.

Jordan busied herself by strolling across the room and studying the wall of photos of past and present Longdale officers.

The precinct door opened. In walked a tiny, little redhead with red lips and red nails. Not to mention curves tight enough to warrant a road hazard sign. Jordan eyeballed little Ms. Cherry-bomb and the designer purse she sauntered in with. Was she going to have to witness one of Ty's *damsels* looking for attention in person?

Jordan checked out her own comfy old hip-huggers with the tear in the knee. She didn't realize Longdale now had a dress code. Cherry-bomb was dressed to kill—tight black slacks, high-heeled boots, short stylish hair, and a great big swagger that sauntered her way too close to Ty.

Jordan spied a badge clipped to the redhead's waist. *Great.* Cherry-bomb was a cop. Interestingly enough, not one Ty had ever mentioned working with.

The redheaded land shark proceeded to stroke a hand down Ty's arm and murmur something Jordan didn't quite catch.

A streak of white-hot fury flashed like a solar flare through Jordan's brain. When your whole life revolved around observing and drawing conclusions, you damn well knew the difference between an innocent hand on your man and one that needed to be cut off and shoved sideways up someone's ass.

Did the woman honestly have no concept of personal space? Who the hell was she, and why the *fuck* was she standing close enough to Ty to count his nose hairs?

Ty glanced between the two females. The silence was deafening except for his abnormally loud attempt at swallowing. No doubt he was choking down the guilty bile that was making his skin take on a sickly green hue.

"Listen, Dale, I'm going to have to call you back." Ty slammed down the phone.

Cherry-bomb whirled around, and Jordan watched the redhead's eyes quickly assess her from top to bottom. "Can I help you?" the woman drawled from her big red painted-on lips.

Jordan edged closer, feeling the need to illustrate what an inappropriate amount of personal space felt like. "I. Very. Seriously. Doubt it." She clenched the paper bag tighter in her hand, trying to decide which one of them she'd like to knock upside the head first.

"Oh, thank God. Lunch," Cherry-bomb said, ripping the bag out of Jordan's hand.

Ty fumbled like a big drunk ape to step between them. "Isobel, would you go wait in my office?"

"Whatever you say, slick." Cherry-bomb winked at Jordan and playfully poked Ty's chest. "This guy will pay you. He owes me a lot more than a sandwich, but I'm going to let him off the hook easy. This time, anyway."

Jordan watched the redhead stroll away with the sandwiches.

Her damn sandwiches.

Finally, she looked over at Ty, really, *really* wanting to rip him a new asshole. But quite honestly, the whole encounter had left her speechless. She didn't know if she was feeling hurt, insult, or jealousy. What she did know was that some suckish emotion was burning through her system at the speed of light.

Ty reached for her hand. "Come here."

She stepped back. Seriously? Was he going to attempt to touch her after that little performance?

Not a chance in hell, cowboy. In fact, the best idea would be to get the hell out of Dodge before her itchy trigger finger went rogue, reached for her Glock, and shot his manhood clean off his guilt-stricken body. "I just swung by to make sure you had lunch. But apparently there's a charming little redhead working here that'll be more than happy to take care of you."

"She's not working here, she's a detective from the Violent Crimes Support Unit of the Missouri Highway Patrol. It wasn't my choice to call her, but we usually need MHP to do all our lab work since we don't have the facilities."

"Meaning she'll be working with you the whole time you're working this case? How nice for you."

He folded his arms over his chest and narrowed his gaze as if she were being ridiculous. "Why do I get the feeling you're angry?"

"Gee, I don't know, Ty." She mirrored his stance, folded her arms, and glared back at him. "Why do I get the feeling you and Cherry-bomb have worked together before?"

"Her name is Isobel Riley." Ty ran his hands through his hair. "And so what? I *have* worked with her before. You've worked with hundreds of different guys. You don't see me making a big deal out of it, because I know you're a professional. Maybe you could treat me with the same respect."

Jordan moved closer now. Not intimately close. Be *very afraid* close. "You wanna play this game with me, cowboy?" she whispered. "You want to pretend that what I just saw between you two was nothing but professional?"

Ty said nothing.

"I don't wear pants tight enough to cut off my air supply while I'm working. I don't wear enough make-up to walk the corner of Washington Street while I'm standing over a crime scene. And I sure as hell don't go around batting my big fake eyelashes and touching the guys I work with. And if I ever do, you should probably make a big deal out of it."

Again he ran his fingers through his hair. Only this time like he wanted to pull most of it out. "Oh, you got it all figured out in the one point five seconds you saw her walk through the room? I had no idea your psychic abilities were anywhere near that sharp."

Jordan stalked to the door, then whipped back around. "I haven't even turned on my psychic radar yet. And trust me, you are *so* not going to like it when I do."

⁂

"That went well," Ty murmured to himself. He squeezed his eyes shut and prayed—*really fucking hard*—that the earth would open up and swallow him whole.

He wanted to be pissed. He wanted to be insulted that Jordan would even suggest that he'd do something sleazy. But the truth of it was that he *had* done something sleazy. Not since he'd been in a relationship with her, of course. But if she pressed for more facts, he wasn't sure how far that sticking point was going to get him.

It was just like a scene from a *National Geographic* special. He was the dumbass, half-wit gazelle about a half a second before it realized it was frolicking through a pack of lions. Instead, he should have been on vacation right now, making love to the long-legged lion with the big breasts and bad temper.

Isobel popped her head out of his office. "Are you about ready to interview David Benson, or what?"

Or what. He really wanted to choose *or what* and go track down Jordan, but David Benson wasn't going to wait forever, and he needed to ask as many questions as possible before the kid lawyered up. He looked at the door Jordan had just stomped out of and then glanced back at Isobel.

Fucking day from hell, that was what this was.

Ty grabbed a couple bottles of water and followed Isobel into the room where David Benson sat staring at the floor.

"Do you mind if I record your statement, David?" Isobel asked.

David turned his glassy red eyes in her direction and gave a small shake of his head. Isobel turned on the recorder, made note of the date, time, and particulars.

"David, do you know this woman?" Isobel scooted a picture of Hailey in front of him.

"Yes."

"What was the nature of your relationship?"

Isobel's tone carried a good amount of unnecessary intimidation, yet Ty let her hammer away at David for several minutes anyway. At least she was establishing a timeline of his history with Hailey. She began to work the details of Friday night, finally getting around to the fight David had with Hailey.

"What was the fight about?" she asked.

David propped his elbows on the table and covered his eyes with his hands. "We were in my bedroom. Just listening to music and stuff. We wanted to be alone, but it was loud in the house and people kept walking past the door, talking and goofing around. So we just went back to the party." David's breath hitched.

"Did you take Hailey to your room with the intention of having sex with her?"

When she asked the question, David's hands fell away from his face and his gaze shot to Isobel's and then to Ty's as if searching for help.

The question had to be asked. Ty knew Isobel could have finessed it a little better. Still he said, "Answer the question, David."

"No," David said. "I mean, nothing was for sure. We just wanted some time alone together."

"And then what happened?" Isobel asked.

"Nothing. It was just so damn noisy. And some jerk came and pounded on the door, just to be an ass, I guess. We decided to go back to the party."

"Did you decide that? Or did Hailey?"

David shrugged.

"We're recording, Mr. Benson, so please answer verbally," Isobel reminded him. She continued the rapid-fire questions. "Were you angry that Hailey decided to go back to the party instead of being alone with you?"

"No," he said. "I mean, I wasn't happy. Mostly frustrated, I guess, because I offered to get us a hotel room."

"So you could have privacy while you had sex with Hailey."

"Yes." David looked at Ty again. "I mean no. You're making it sound like I was pressuring her to do something, but I wasn't. She wanted to be with me, too. We were just trying to figure out . . ." David pressed the heels of his hands into his eyes. "I loved her. I swear I'd never do anything she didn't want me to do."

"But you *were* angry that she changed her mind about having sex Friday night?"

"I was frustrated, okay? She was always so busy ... We both were. She said she couldn't skip the party because she was a chaperone for one of the freshman."

"A chaperone?" Isobel challenged.

"They do this thing in her sorority where every freshman gets paired up with an upperclassman. Kind of a buddy system so none of the girls get too drunk or taken advantage of. I just wanted one night where it wasn't about school, family, or sorority crap."

"Did the fight turn physical?"

"What? No," David said. "There wasn't really even a fight. I told you, I'd never hurt Hailey." David got very quiet. Tears started running down his face again. "Oh God, you think I killed her, don't you? I swear I didn't." He leaned toward Ty. "I loved her. I picked out a ring to give her when school was over this summer. I already made the first payment. I can't believe she's gone," he sobbed.

"No one is accusing you of killing her, David." Ty narrowed his eyes at Isobel, knowing full well that was exactly the road she was barreling down. "In order to find who did this, we need a timeline so we understand everything that happened in her life. Right up until the last minute."

"What happened when the fight ended, David?" he asked.

"I went to the basement and played poker." David's gaze met Ty's. "And I drank. I'm so stupid. I loved her, and I could have spent a few more hours with her, but I didn't. I should have been there to walk her home. If I'd done that, she'd still be alive, wouldn't she?"

Ty watched the tears flood down David's cheeks.

"Every relationship has fights," he said. He thought about Jordan storming out of his office a little while ago. "But it really is better to tell us everything now. If we find out later that you lied, then it looks like you had something to hide."

"When was the last time you saw Hailey alive?" Isobel jumped in again.

"I told you. Before she left the frat house," David mumbled.

"What time was it?"

David shrugged. "I don't know. I can't do this anymore." David dropped his head on the table. "I want my dad. Please, I just want my dad."

Ty tried to calm David a couple more times, but David just kept crying and asking for his dad. They were walking a fine line between witness and suspect, and Ty didn't want to jeopardize the case. He followed Isobel out of the interview room.

"See, this is why I told you to read him his rights," Isobel said.

"I had no plans to arrest him, Isobel. I just wanted to know what happened. And he'd have told us a hell of a lot more if you hadn't scared the shit out of him."

"More lies, you mean?"

Ty folded his arms. "I didn't get the feeling he was lying. He's so hungover he can't even think straight, much less form a decent lie."

"Are you kidding?" Isobel tossed her hands up. "A rich, spoiled kid like that, completely used to having his way and getting exactly what he wants? Except he didn't get Hailey, and he was pissed about it. He told us that much himself."

"That doesn't mean he killed her. And if you'd backed off a bit, he probably would have been more open about what happened next instead of asking for his dad. Which is just the same as asking for a lawyer."

"So let him get a lawyer. I'm checking on the warrants to search his frat room and car. And if we find any piece of evidence or get another witness to remember any violence between them, I'm going to the DA."

"I think that might be premature, Isobel."

Isobel's expression turned softer, almost like she took pity on him. "That's because you're a good guy from small town, USA. I've dealt with his kind, Ty. Wealthy, arrogant, making a lifelong career out of lying and avoiding any responsibility. I agree we don't have enough on him yet. Let's see what the search turns up."

Isobel pranced away, and Ty got the feeling he'd just been called a dumbass hillbilly in the nicest of ways. Apparently one of them was a dumbass, because they weren't seeing eye to eye regarding David Benson. Despite the drinking and the fight with Hailey, he didn't think those things added up to David being a murderer. Then again, he'd also thought he could keep Jordan and Isobel from ever crossing paths, and look how well that turned out.

Jordan used the one-and-a-half-hour drive to Saunders Funeral Home in St. Louis to calm herself.

Damn men.

Why did relationships have to screw with your head so badly? Since when had she become such a jealous idiot?

She glanced in the rear-view mirror. Her hair was in a ponytail. No make-up to speak of. Jeans, boots, an old jacket. Okay, so she did look more like a sandwich delivery girl than a cop. But Cherry-bomb certainly didn't ooze professionalism, either. Seriously, who investigated a murder wearing fuck-me-red lipstick?

Someone who wanted to fuck a big rugged cop like Ty, *that's who.*

"Okay, enough," she chastised herself. None of this was Ty's fault. She couldn't act like an idiot every time an attractive woman flirted with him.

Ty wasn't a liar.

And he wasn't a cheater.

By the time she pulled into the parking lot of the funeral home, she decided she owed him an apology. And how the hell that had happened, she had no idea.

Damn relationships.

She turned off the car and looked around. So this was it? She'd worked so close for so many years and never had a clue that graves for her family were just around the corner?

In less than fifteen minutes, she walked out of the funeral home with a map of the huge cemetery and a sick feeling in the pit of her stomach. It had taken a few little white lies and a wave of her badge, but she'd also managed to harass the timid clerk into giving her a plot number where Jack Delany had been buried.

This certainly wasn't how she'd pictured the last few days of her vacation. Visions of sand and ocean and sipping frosty little drinks while Ty rubbed lotion all over her body was a much nicer image. She was a long, *long* way from that fantasy.

The narrow blacktop road twisted and curved toward a large lake and the spot the clerk had marked on the map. She parked, got out, and leaned back against her car. The snow accumulation was barely a dusting here. Acre after acre of headstones and flowers peeked up through the thin layer of white. Kind of gruesomely beautiful, really.

But she sensed very little energy. Seemed the dead didn't like hanging out in cemeteries any more than the living.

She'd been to rock concerts where she sensed more spirit. Yet it made perfect sense. If a soul could bounce around anywhere, a sandy beach in Jamaica had to beat the hell out of a depressing grave in Missouri.

If some drug dealer eventually put a bullet in her, she had no intention of hovering over a cold chunk of stone when her spirit could instead invisibly ogle Ty in a warm shower.

She closed her eyes and attempted to mentally prepare for whatever lay across the road. Graves or no graves, it shouldn't matter. *This* shouldn't matter. Her family had been gone for twenty years.

So why did she feel like she was losing them all over again?

She pushed off her car, but her feet didn't seem to be on board with the need to move. Maybe because she couldn't think past the memory that kept looping over and over in her mind—her uncle's blue and white pontoon boat.

Certain days leave an imprint, much like a brand on the brain. Time had never dulled the memories of spreading ashes of her mom, dad, and Katy.

The sun had been bright, but the cold, windy day had bit at her cheeks like a million stinging bees. Her stomach was sick, and the throbbing in her head intensified with the speed of the boat.

She had once loved that lake. Her family had, too. However she had never been out on the water when no one else was around.

It was the wrong time of year for boating.

A box sat next to her. Her uncle had explained that it contained three urns. Until that day, she hadn't known what the word *urn* had meant. The vibrations of the boat made the metal urns clank together.

The clearest memory was how unfathomable it had been that her entire family, three whole people, fit inside a small box with room to spare. Her whole world had been in that box. And she watched that world float away in the waves in the lake.

Maybe. But maybe not. If Bahan were correct, it seemed that might be another fact up for debate.

No, absolutely not. She refused to believe it. For years she'd resented her uncle for not taking her in when her family had been murdered. She considered him a major asshole for that, but even he couldn't be cruel enough to stage the spreading of ashes for his own family.

She cleared her mind and forced herself away from the car. Counting the rows and headstones, she came upon . . .

Jack Edmund Delany.

After reading the documents in her father's file, she'd expected a headstone with her father's name on it, had steeled herself for it. She just hadn't expected the sick roll of her stomach, as though she were still on that damn pontoon boat.

Her throat swelled and burned.

Her eyes stung.

"I'm sorry, Dad," she whispered. "I don't even know how to ask for forgiveness. I've managed to find the truth for complete strangers, but you . . . I never did for you. Now I will. I promise."

She glanced at the next headstone. *Mary Elizabeth Delany.* Her mom.

Rein it in, Jordan. This can't be real. Even so, the third headstone was a bitter pill. *Jordan Miranda Delany, June 30, 1983 – November 25, 1993.*

A cruel irony swallowed her up, because she couldn't say that the date of her death was wrong. Anything she had been before November 25, 1993 was a hell of a long way from everything she'd become after.

But seeing the headstone with her name on it was almost a relief, assurance that all of this really was just an elaborate setting. She wasn't, after all, dead. For certain, at least one of the graves was empty. In her heart she believed the other three were, as well.

Then she read the fourth gravestone. *Kathleen Janet Delany.*

Katy.

Her Katy.

She turned from the graves and tried to suck air back into her lungs. She bent forward, propped her hands on her knees, and let her head hang.

This is just another lie someone created. An extensive lie, but a lie nonetheless.

Her little sister had never belonged to her mom and dad. Katy was hers, her bad guy to tie up or her doll to dress. Her partner in crime. An easy victim to point the finger at when Mom was pissed because crap ended up broken. A sloppy little roommate who would crawl into bed with her when the dreams got bad.

The same frigid tears from all those years ago streaked down her cheeks. She turned back to Katy's grave. The ground was damp and slushy, and still she knelt and brushed dead leaves and snow from around Katy's headstone. Her left hand smoothed over the carved letters of her own name; her right hand traced Katy's name. When would the one spirit she really wanted to hear from ever come through?

Katy had called out for her just seconds before the last gunshot rang out. Of all the things Jordan regretted, not opening that closet door and going to Katy was at the top of the list.

"I'm sorry, Katy. I really am. If I could change what I did that night and be with you, I would."

She had no idea if Katy could hear her, because unlike her parents, Katy was still holding a grudge. She had been since the night of the murders.

"Why won't you talk to me? Dad tries to talk to me in my dreams all the time. Hell, I can't get Ty's sister to ever shut up. Why can't you forgive me and show up in a dream just once? One time, that's all I'm asking."

An older man with a long beard walked by and looked over at her. Embarrassed, Jordan swiped at the tears and stood. She was pleading with her dead sister. Beard guy probably thought she'd lost her mind.

Actually, she did feel a bit like she was losing her mind. She had to know if her family was here or if this was just a charade that had been put in place to protect her. She looked down at the graves, determined to see them for nothing more than the cover-up they were.

She'd spread her family's ashes, said goodbye to them that day on her uncle's boat. This... *this* couldn't be anything more than a farce. But how could she prove it? There were laws against exhuming graves, even for cops. She'd have to get a lawyer and go before a judge. And screwing around with graves that the Feds had made a public production out of would be trickier yet.

There was, however, one person who could clear everything up without any of that hassle.

Her uncle Bill.

Too bad she'd sworn to never speak to the son of a bitch again.

She swiped at her wet, dirty knees, and snapped pictures of each of the headstones with her cellphone. The answers were out there. The real answers. She had a right to know what her father had been working on and why he'd been killed. And she had a right to know if she really had spread her family's ashes, or if it was one more lie she'd been told.

CHAPTER 5

Ty drove through the gate of the ranch he shared with Jordan. Just the sight of their new property gave him a feeling of pride and contentment he'd never experienced before. The house needed work and the stables needed work. But he remembered what the place had looked like in its heyday. Jordan was going to love it when he was done.

Maybe a little more than she loved him right at the moment. She'd been pissed when she left the precinct earlier. It had taken her about two seconds to zero in on Isobel's behavior. Seemed living with a psychic detective apparently didn't give you much wiggle room to make dumb guy mistakes.

As predicted, he was running almost an hour late. So he'd called Jordan to make sure she was ready.

She was waiting for him on the porch as he pulled up. She climbed into his black F-350 and they took off toward his parents' house.

"Look," he said, "I want to explain about the female detective you saw today." There was no point in delaying the inevitable. Jordan wasn't stupid.

She sighed and held up her hand.

He paused, wasn't quite sure what to make of her gesture.

"Let me start by saying I'm sorry. I know you don't control who MHP sends to help with cases. I walked into your office and behaved like a jealous child." She reached over and lightly traced a finger over the back of his hand. "You had a long, stressful day, and I made it worse. You've never given me any reason to doubt you."

A bitter laugh erupted from her. "But in my defense, I've warned you that I suck at relationships." Her thumb rubbed a soft little circle on the back of his hand. "I suppose the only thing I can do now is try to make it up to you somehow."

Great. Now he felt like a real dickhead. "Well, to tell you the truth . . ." He glanced at her without turning his head.

She laced her fingers with his, lifted their hands, and kissed the back of his. Then she teased him by gently sucking on his index finger.

His heart rate spiked.

He hadn't done anything wrong, but figured it might be a good idea to come clean before they went any farther.

"I just think you should understand—"

"I do understand. You're a good-looking guy. Women are going to come on to you. I get it. And I know in my heart you're not stupid enough to sleep with a co-worker, even if I wasn't in the picture."

She sighed. "Just don't be mad at me while we're at your parents. I can't take that. I'm already nervous as hell."

"Baby, I'm not mad." He squeezed *her* hand this time. "And you have nothing to be nervous about. They'll love you." He paused for a second, then decided to attempt to put her at ease regarding his parents before stirring her up about Issy. "They already like you. A lot. I told them you were the one responsible for me being able to catch the guy who killed Tara."

Jordan pulled her hand away from his. "What? You didn't tell them how, did you?"

"Of course not. Just that you were another cop who helped me."

"What am I supposed to say if they start asking questions about how I helped?"

He shrugged. "Tell them we can't talk about the specifics of the case. Or that you're uncomfortable talking about cases with family members of the victims. Or . . ." He glanced at her again. "We could tell them the truth."

"Funny. You're funny."

He stopped at a light and glanced over at her. "I'm not trying to be. I'm serious. Losing Tara was awful. I still miss her, but knowing she's around sometimes makes it . . . I don't know, tolerable somehow. I'd do anything to make it tolerable for my parents."

Her mouth dropped open.

Okay, not a good sign.

"You are *not* serious. You do *not* expect me to go in there and say, 'Hi. Nice to meet you. By the way I've connected with your dead daughter and she's doing fine.' Why don't you just burn me at the stake now, ensure your entire family thinks I'm a nut job from the very beginning. And guess what?" She poked him in the arm. "You just moved in with me, so they're going to think you're as crazy as I am. Trust me on this. Sometimes it's kinder all around to spare everyone the ugly truth."

He had never been a good liar, wasn't brought up to hide the truth from the people he loved, even if it was ugly. But maybe Jordan was right. Maybe some truths were better left unsaid. Like the fact that Jordan communicated with the dead.

And the fact he'd slept with Isobel.

He was beginning to see the wisdom in her logic. As he turned onto the long gravel drive to his parents' house, he decided that at the very least, both conversations were going to have to wait. "Whatever you say, baby. Whatever you say."

Ty's mom was attractive, almost elegant with her height, long limbs, and willowy figure. She wore a simple pink blouse and jeans. Jordan immediately classified her as one of *those* women, the kind other women noticed. And envied. Her dark hair was bobbed with simple elegance. Her accessories were stylish. Even her nails were manicured to perfection.

But it was her eyes that Jordan couldn't stop studying, the darkness that shadowed them and the red rims that no amount of expensive make-up could ever cover. They were the same striking gray as Ty's, only they'd long since surrendered the humor and mischief.

"Mom, this is Jordan," Ty said. "Jordan, my mom, Maggie."

Maggie took her hand and pulled her into a quick hug. "I'm so glad to meet you. Ty has told us so many good things. And he sure didn't lie about how pretty you are."

Embarrassed, Jordan waved a dismissive hand in Ty's direction. "Oh well, he tends to exaggerate."

"And you already know Trevor," Ty said, when his brother approached.

"Hi, beautiful." Trevor kissed her cheek.

"You've already met Jordan? When did that happen? Why don't you boys tell me anything?" Ty's mom asked.

Jordan recognized Trevor's shit-eating grin and knew he was about to say something obnoxious about their first encounter. She'd made a grand ass of herself by walking out of the bathroom buck naked with the intent to seduce Ty. Only it hadn't been Ty crouched in the corner of their bedroom trying to fix the radiator. It had been Trevor.

"Let's see?" Trevor tapped a finger against his chin. "When did we meet for the first time? Oh, yes, it's coming back to me now. Ty asked me to come over and help fix the radiators in their house. I started in their bedroom first, and—"

"And that was it. End of story." Ty shot Trevor a warning glare.

Red-hot humiliation flamed in Jordan's cheeks. It hadn't been one of her finer moments.

"What?" Trevor's voice dripped with mock innocence. "I was just explaining to Mom how Jordan introduced herself to me. And I assure you, Ty does not exaggerate about Jordan's beauty."

Maggie rolled her eyes. "Come on into the kitchen. I've got rolls in the oven."

When Maggie turned around, Ty whacked Trevor on the back of the head like they were twelve.

"So Mom said you're working a murder? That's why you're late?" Trevor asked as they turned to follow Maggie.

"He says it was the case that held him up. I think it may have been the redhead who clearly has a thing for him." Jordan teased.

Trevor's gaze snapped to Ty's. "*The* redhead? The one from the highway patrol? Holy crap, she's back?"

Jordan stopped, and both guys halted in her tracks. She studied Ty and then Trevor. The uncomfortable tension told her that Tinkerbelle, or Annabelle, or whatever the fuck her name was, had been a topic of discussion before. If Trevor's insinuating words hadn't been the tipping point, the furious, guilty look on Ty's face certainly would have been.

She stood in silence and waited for Ty to say something.

He managed to look everywhere except in her direction.

"I need to use the restroom," she murmured. But just barely. A miserable, grinding burn was spreading through her chest and making it ridiculously hard to speak. She'd stood over graves containing the names of her family today and hadn't felt an ache this vicious.

"I'll show you where it is." Ty reached for her hand.

"I can find it." She blinked away the ludicrous sting and arrowed toward the restroom. She knew the way. On their last case, she'd spent more than a week here recovering from injuries while Ty's parents vacationed in Florida.

She certainly couldn't control who Ty had or had not been with. No doubt he'd had sex with many women before her. He was too damn good at it to not have had a lot of practice.

But her heart told her that he'd lied today. Or at the very least, omitted the truth. From her experience, when a suspect omitted an important truth in interrogation, there was always a reason. Usually not a good one.

Like maybe he still had feelings for the redhead.

As she suspected he might, he followed her inside the small bathroom and shut the door behind them.

"Uh, I don't need an audience, thanks."

"Don't listen to Trevor," he said. "You know how he is, always joking around—"

"Did you have a relationship with her?" *God*, she hated that she felt like this. Simply *hated* that she blurted that question out.

"No. It wasn't like that . . ."

"Okay, then, let me ask this to clear the record. The redhead I saw in your precinct today, the one that grabbed the sandwiches out of my hands and said you'd pay because you *owed* her—*that one*—have you had sex with her?"

He didn't answer.

Which in itself was answer enough. Her throat swelled even tighter, and although she was fighting the burning sensation with everything she had, her eyes welled up.

"I'll tell my mom I got a call from the station about the case and we can't stay," he said.

"No, you won't." No way in hell was she doing the meet-the-parent thing twice. She hadn't been ready for this, and he'd insisted on dragging her here, anyway. So he could sit and be just as miserable as she was.

"Your mom probably cooked and cleaned, going to a lot of trouble for tonight. It's not her fault you're a jackass. We're both going to go in there and be pleasant, make small talk, and get through this."

She opened the bathroom door and pushed him out. "But if I were you, I wouldn't hold my breath for a massage or any other form of physical contact for a very long time. At least not from me. You might have better luck with the redhead."

Ty sat at his mom and dad's dinner table staring at his favorite pot roast in misery. He glanced across the table at Trevor. The dumbass seemed to recognize he was going to get his ass kicked as soon as they were alone together. They were both just pushing their food around.

On top of it all, their dad wasn't even making an effort. He'd decided to live in misery since the day he learned of Tara's murder. As far as anyone could tell, he had depression down to a science. The man hardly spoke anymore. Ty had no idea how his mom put up with it. He was a little ticked off that his dad hadn't at least tried to be sociable with Jordan.

Jordan had done just what she'd said she would. She'd been funny, polite, answered all questions with a smile. It was like she'd flipped a switch in that damn bathroom and decided to be nothing less than charming. *Except* when it came to interacting with him. The one time he laid a hand on her thigh under the table, she'd almost twisted his thumb clean off.

"Would anyone like more rolls?" his mom asked.

"Thank you, but I'm stuffed. It was wonderful, though," Jordan said. "Ty will probably sneak over here a lot to eat. I'm a horrible cook. I work a lot of hours and have never really gotten the hang of it."

"I haven't cooked much the last year, either," his mom answered. "This was nice. I really enjoyed having the whole family here."

Ty's dad dropped his fork and turned immediately to the one empty chair. Tara's chair. "It was nice to meet you, Jordan," he said. "If you'll excuse me, I've got to finish feeding the horses and take care of some things out in the barn."

"It was nice to meet you, too." Jordan smiled at him. "You should come out to our stable and help Ty figure out what needs to be done to get the place functioning again."

His dad pushed back from the table and stood. "You planning on having horses out there?"

"Maybe," Ty answered. "Haven't decided yet."

"That would be good. You could take your horses, then. I just can't see us keeping this farm and all the land. Time to think about retiring, not about what crop gets planted next."

Ty's mom stood and nailed his dad with a dangerous glare. "Give it a rest, Rick. We are *not* selling this farm."

His dad turned and walked out without another word. Couldn't the man have made an effort for one frigging night? Right about now, Jordan was probably thankful she didn't have any family to deal with.

"I'm gonna go talk to him," Trevor said.

Ty wasn't sure whether to follow Trevor or stay with the women.

Jordan eventually graced him with a look. Not a particularly affectionate one. "Why don't you go with them?"

"I thought maybe you'd like me to stay—"

She narrowed her eyes. "Don't be silly. Go talk with Trevor and your dad. I certainly don't need you."

Jordan watched Ty sulk out of the kitchen.

The ass-hat.

Still, she couldn't help feeling sorry for him. The energy in the room told her everyone was still trying to recover from Tara's death. But while Trevor, Ty, and Maggie seemed to be coming around, Ty's dad, on the other hand, was struggling big time.

The hole that death left took time to fill again. She knew that better than anyone. And murder left a particularly wide and vicious hole. Tara had been murdered less than a year ago, so all of them would still have bad days.

"I'm sorry." Ty's mom dropped down into a chair and looked at Jordan as though she wanted to crawl under the table and curl into a ball. "This is the first meal we've had as a family since Tara's been gone. I thought he could handle it. This was my fault; I was the one who insisted we do this." Tears began to swim in Maggie's eyes.

Hells bells, what a fucked-up day. Jordan had let deception and lies screw with her for more years than she cared to think about. She might as well let the truth yank her around for a while. "Has Ty told you anything about my family?"

Maggie met Jordan's gaze and shook her head.

"My dad, my mom, and my sister were murdered when I was ten," Jordan admitted quietly. "I was in the house when it happened. I only survived because I was hiding in a closet."

Maggie's eyes widened, but instead of speaking, she lightly squeezed Jordan's wrist.

They sat in silence for a long quiet moment. As uncomfortable as it should have been, strangely it wasn't uncomfortable at all. Jordan supposed nothing bonded strangers quite like sharing a horrible, murder-filled past.

"I would never recommend two people meeting the way Ty and I did, but as unfortunate as they were, our pasts are one link that makes us understand each other so well."

Ty's mom broke. "I miss her. Every minute of every day. I just can't live in the isolation that Rick wants to live in. I miss my boys. I miss cooking for them and having family dinners. I miss going to church. I miss my stupid part-time job at the flower shop."

Jordan felt Tara's presence sweep through the kitchen like a wild, whirling twister. *Tell her. Tell her I'm okay. Tell her to be happy, I want her to be happy.*

Jordan sucked in a breath. Tara was a force she couldn't deny.

To appear normal to the living, Jordan blocked all communication with spirits during the day. In the night, she let them come, tell her what they needed her to know. But the daytime hours were hers, and the spirits seemed to understand that.

Except for Tara.

She had never been able to block Ty's little sister because . . . Hell, she wasn't even sure why. Maybe because she liked the girl. Tara had helped Jordan save Ty's life. A little sister spirit was all around Jordan when Tara was near. After losing Katy, there was something about Tara's spirit that was comforting.

This situation, however, was *not* comfortable.

"Rick makes it sound like I'm betraying Tara if I do anything. It's making me crazy. He wanted to have the boys sell the farm while we stayed in Florida. He never wanted to come back. How could he not want to come back? This is home."

They don't have to sell the farm. They love the farm. Tell her I'm okay.

Nothing like juggling competing conversations in your head at the same time. Tara's thoughts were overlapping with Maggie's words, and the tension . . . God, the tension was making it hard to breathe.

"This was Tara's home," Maggie sobbed. "I'll never leave."

Tell her. Tell her I'm still with her and always will be. Why won't you tell her?

"Tara, stop it." Jordan spoke louder than she'd meant to.

Maggie's gaze whipped toward her.

"Not you." Jordan looked at Maggie, mortified. "I mean . . . Well, see, what I meant is that I think Tara would want you to stop feeling that way. I don't think she'd want your life to come to a screeching halt. Ty has told me what a sweet, loving girl she was."

Please tell her I want her to be happy.

"Maggie, whether Tara is here or in the next world, you'd always want her to be happy, right?"

Maggie nodded and dabbed her eyes with a tissue.

"I don't think she would want any less for you."

Jordan wondered if her mom and dad were rolling in their graves from the irony. She was pretty sure they had tried to communicate that same fact for the last twenty years, only she had just never gotten it. It had taken Ty's sister to drive the point home.

Ty's mom's eyes widened, and her face went white.

"I can't believe I just sat here and unloaded on you like this." She swiped the tears from her cheeks. "Ty is such a good man. Please don't let tonight and all our issues scare you off. I can see in his eyes what you mean to him."

Jordan almost laughed. "It would take a lot more than what happened here tonight to scare me off. And if you tell Ty I said that, I will flat out deny it." She shot Maggie an amused smile. "I'm usually the mental charity case that Ty gently tolerates. It's kind of nice to know the tables can turn once in a while."

Maggie smiled. "Somehow, I doubt that he has to put up with you. I'm just sorry tonight didn't turn out quite like I'd hoped."

Now, here, with all of Ty's family, Jordan realized just how many years she'd spent in selfish isolation. Ty was the first person who had ever made her feel that she wasn't suffering alone. Maybe if she had ever bothered to look around and help someone else before tonight, the bitter knot in her own chest would have loosened sooner.

"I know what losing someone to murder does to you," she said. "You don't ever have to apologize for your reactions. Not to me, anyway."

CHAPTER 6

On the way home, Ty kept glancing over at Jordan sitting beside him in the truck.

Both of them preferred a balls-to-the-wall knock-down-drag-out to the silent treatment. Which, he figured, was precisely the reason she was ignoring the hell out of him.

"There's a good ice cream shop about a half mile from here. You want dessert since dinner was kind of a bust?"

"No. I'm good." She never looked up from her phone.

He knew damn well there wasn't anything on it interesting enough to keep her from speaking. "So I got the feeling you wanted to talk to me about something when you came by the office today."

"Nothing that can't wait until your case is over."

"Come on, what was it?"

She shrugged. "Bahan came over. He brought my dad's file. Confirmed my dad was undercover for the FBI when his cover was blown. Someone from a drug cartel murdered my family—the same cartel Arlo and Warren Buck were working for on our last case."

The air caught in his chest. Her news was a huge fucking deal, and she hadn't said a thing. "Holy shit." He reached for her hand. "Why didn't you say anything?"

They were stopped at a four-way stop. She shot him the Jordan Delany death stare. "I came to your office right after Bahan left, but you had your hands full. Remember?"

No way was he wiggling out of this one. A car behind him honked, and he stomped on the gas. "Fine, if you're pissed about Isobel, let's have it out now and move on."

"Gee, Ty," she said, "I was talking about the murder you caught this morning. Funny how your mind jumped right to Isobel. Why do you feel like your hands are full because of her? Maybe because you banged her?"

He blew through the narrow gate of their ranch and stopped in front of the house. Jordan jumped out of the truck as if it were on fire and bolted inside. He followed her, praying that the day would end soon. Or that someone would just end him. Either option worked.

Jordan was already halfway up the stairs. He stomped up behind her, followed her into the bedroom. "You want the truth. Yes, I slept with her. One time. One night. We parted ways and that was it. It was no big deal."

She brushed past him with a disgusted shake of her head. "I *really* thought you were smarter than that."

"Are you going to stand there and tell me that you've never had sex with another cop you were working with? Not one time? Not one slip-up?"

When she whirled around and stepped toward him, he realized the look she'd given him in the truck was just a warmup.

"Yes, I'm going to stand here and tell you in no uncertain terms that I have never, *ever*, slept with another cop. That I have never slept with anyone that I've worked with. And then I'm going to tell you why."

She moved closer and jabbed a finger into his chest. "Because I've worked my ass off since day one in that fucking academy. I was one of three women in a group of thirty-five men. Two days before I graduated, I was asked to participate in an undercover op and I've never looked back. And I will be damned if one fucking man is ever going to say I earned my cases or my rank because I slept with the right guy."

"Really? 'Cause you slept with me."

Her whole body jolted back in surprise.

With every fiber of his being he wanted to grab the words and yank them back. In all honesty, he preferred seeing anger in her expression to the hurt.

"I slept with you because for the first time since my family was gone, I felt something that I didn't know how to turn away from. Is that what it was between you and Isobel?"

He scrubbed his hands up and down his face. "Of course not. She came on to me after a long draining case. We arrested a guy for killing a little kid, and we were both feeling kind of . . . raw. Reckless, I guess. We went to a bar, had a few beers. I slept with her one time and never saw her again."

Jesus, he was tired. He trudged to the end of the bed and sat. "In Longdale, we're just a handful of country cops, and no one gives a shit about rank or who you sleep with. We don't have a team of detectives, or a separate vice unit, or drug team; we do it all. And when something big happens, highway patrol gets involved."

Jordan sat next to him. "I know you've slept with other women, and I don't care about what happened in your past. I don't care if you've been with ten other cops. But you tried to hide it today. That tells me there was more to it back then . . ."

When her voice trailed off he knew, just fucking knew, what she was implying.

". . . and maybe there's more to it now."

He stood and stomped away because the only other option was to go postal. Only Jordan could draw such a fucked-up line from point A to point B. How the hell could she *still* doubt what was between them?

"I don't even know what to say to that. There wasn't really time to explain a one-night stand with Isobel in the two minutes you stopped by my office. And this conversation"—he motioned between them—"right here? This is exactly why I didn't offer up the information. I had a brief encounter with her that lasted roughly as long as it takes to brush your teeth and wasn't quite as exciting. Oh, screw it. I'm taking a shower."

He stripped, walked to the bathroom door, and then turned back. "I'm not gonna lie, I've have had sex with a lot of women. But I've only ever been in love with one. Let me know if you ever figure out the math."

How did he always do something completely stupid and then make her feel like *she* was the idiot? Of course, he had to go and say something that made her whole chest ache. How could she stay mad with him being so . . . so Ty?

Plus he'd walked past her buck naked. It would be a whole lot easier to stay pissed if he wasn't built like a god.

The ass.

Maybe she *was* an idiot, but the thought of going to bed while they were still mad at each other made a dull ache settle in her stomach. In the short time they'd been together, she'd become shamelessly dependent on having him wrapped around her at night. She'd slept better in the last few months than she ever had.

She blew out a giant sigh and flopped back on the bed. Navigating a relationship wasn't her specialty. Maybe there were times when she needed to suck up her pride and apologize. Times like tonight.

After peeling out of her clothes, she went into the bathroom and stepped into the shower behind him.

His big arm was propped against the wall and his head was hanging down. Steamy water trailed along the muscles in his back. It was embarrassing how fiercely her body responded to the sight of his. In awe of the picture he made, she laid her hands on his back and then smoothed them up to his shoulders and squeezed.

"I'm sorry," she said.

After pumping out a few handfuls of soap, she massaged it over his back. The tension in his shoulders eased. Ironically, her insides began to coil tightly.

She remembered the first time she'd felt the sensation.

The very first night she met him, he turned to walk away and her body had physically ached with something so unfamiliar she had no words to describe it. Nothing much was different now. Except that now she recognized the sensation to be so much more than the simple lust she first dismissed it as.

"Nothing pisses me off more than you doubting how I feel about you," he murmured through the steam and the water.

"I know. I don't doubt you, and I don't want to fight." She also didn't doubt that Isobel Riley wanted him, but it was time to let that go before she caused more damage to their relationship than Isobel ever would. She slid her arms around his waist, lowered her hand to stroke him, and found him steel-hard already. Fighting didn't appear to be top on his priority list, either. She pumped her fingers up and down his length until all the muscles in his back tightened again.

He groaned and spun around, then lowered his lips to the curve of her neck and licked all the way up to her ear. *God*, there was just something about the way Tyler McGee used his tongue that made all of her bones turn to liquid.

Placing a hand under her knee, he lifted her leg and propped her foot on the edge of the shower seat. He opened her, gently teasing her clit with one clever finger before spearing it inside her.

"Ty," she cried out, arching against his hand. She wrapped an arm around his neck and brought his mouth to hers. His tongue moved and teased just as shrewdly as his fingers. In and out. In and out. An erotic rhythm causing a deep thrumming pleasure to pulse from her core.

She wanted to touch him. Needed to touch him. Now. Right now. She ran an unsteady hand down his chest, down his stomach, straight down to his shaft with the intention of gently stroking him. But he tightened his big hand over hers and urged her into a tighter, quicker rhythm.

When his mouth moved back to her neck, his breath rushed in and out. He added another finger to the one already inside her and rolled the pad of his thumb around and around her clit.

Not to be outdone, she fisted her hand up and down his length until he groaned against her ear.

He moved his hand away, and she thought she might lose her mind. She wanted to scream, wanted to beg. "Please," she ended up whispering. They both had to be just seconds away from . . .

He caught her thighs, pinned her ass against the wall, and drove inside her.

The orgasm ripped through her the second he sank in. "Thank God. Oh, thank God." She was vaguely aware of the gasping chant rising from her chest, but damned if she could quiet it. Her fingers clenched in the dark silk of his hair and held on while her body continued to vibrate and splinter.

It was as near a religious experience as she'd ever come. If heaven offered anything close to the blinding orgasms Ty delivered, there wouldn't be so many spirits driving her crazy at night.

Still, she hung on. Wrung out. Breathless.

"Again," he growled, never slowing the pace. Faster. Harder. Deeper with every thrust. "Again," he demanded.

Too sensitive and too spent, she knew she couldn't come again so soon, but the determination in his voice warmed her veins like an expensive shot of tequila. Damned if her body didn't begin to tighten a second time.

Okay then. Hell, yes, again.

She thought the words, couldn't begin to speak them through the tight clench of her lungs. The hot water heated her skin until she was mere seconds from combustion. Clenched muscles in her arms and legs burned with the exertion of clinging to him.

But her core, her core raced, begged, pleaded for another release.

"Come for me, baby. One more time. Squeeze that pretty body around me over and over, *Oh God, yes. I fucking love that . . . ohhh . . .*"

His erotic plea drop-kicked her into another vicious climax. That and feeling his huge body pound hot and wild inside her. She pulled his mouth to hers and devoured him until he drew back for air.

"Holy shit." His breath heaved in and out. He flipped them so that his back was leaning against the wall. Then, like the rivulets of water, they slid down and onto the shower floor. "Holy fucking shit," he grumbled against her neck again.

She laughed. Neither of them were poets, but Ty's words pretty well summed up the moment.

After a minute or two, he opened his eyes and looked at her. "Did we just have make-up sex?"

"Not sure." She was still wrapped around him, straddling him on the shower floor as hot water sprayed around them. "I think we just had *I'm going to look past your tumble with Skanky-bell but if you touch her again I will cut your nuts off* sex."

He chuckled. "Fair enough." He brushed the wet hair back off her face. "You can't logically believe after the last ten minutes that there's any chance I'd look at another woman."

"Since when has logic ever entered into this thing between you and me?"

"True." His head dropped back against the shower wall. "Although right now, I can't even stand up. How the hell do you think I'd have the energy to juggle two of you?"

She narrowed her eyes but couldn't help grinning at the jerk. His smartass statement touched off an idea that wasn't half bad. Another round or two of sex like the one they'd just had, and she was quite certain he wouldn't have the energy to get out of bed in the morning, much less give anyone else a second glance.

"I'm just saying that maybe whatever happened between you and the redhead didn't mean anything to you, but I have eyes. Skanky-belle wants a round two with you." Afraid she might be on the verge of heatstroke, she scooted back and reached up to adjust the water temperature.

Ty cupped her breasts as she fiddled with the nozzle. "In my own twisted way, I find it kind of hot that you're jealous and all. I just think you might want to be jealous over someone I actually wanted a round one with."

"Not helping." She wrapped her hand around his dick and gave it a warning squeeze. "Just remember, I own this. Don't you ever forget it."

He surprised her by pulling her close for a soft, tender kiss. Then he lifted her hand and laid it on his chest, right over his heart. "*This* is the body part you own. And don't *you* ever forget it."

CHAPTER 7

"Die?" The girl mumbled the word as tears and blood streaked down her face. "What are you talking about? You've had too much to drink. David, you're scaring me."

Casually, he shrugged. Then pulled the blue baseball cap down tighter on his mop of blond hair. "I haven't had a drop of alcohol."

He stepped closer.

She scrambled to her feet and backed away.

"Do I look drunk, Hailey? Do I talk like I'm drunk?"

"I know you're drunk. I saw how much you had to drink tonight." She turned to run.

He lunged, slamming her face first into the snow, then flipped her over.

"David, stop," she cried as he pinned her arms to the ground. "Don't do this! We can fix whatever is wrong."

"No, we can't.*" He straddled her body and moved one hand to her slender throat. "But I can."*

An odd sensation made Jordan blink her eyes open. Her hands and feet were frigid, but her lungs were on fire. She drew in a greedy breath—once, twice—and then it happened again. A moist, rough lick streaked up the side of her cheek. Warm breath panted in her ear. Unless Ty was trying some different moves to pull her out of a dream, she suspected—actually, hoped like hell—Beauty was sharing some affection.

She reared back in her desk chair.

Beauty scurried away and whined.

"It's okay, girl. I'm fine." She reached out to reassure the dog. "You'll get used to it."

The dog cocked her head as if challenging Jordan. Beauty was wise beyond her years. "Okay, you may not get used to it, but you'll cope. If I can, and Ty can, then you can, too."

Of course, last night she hadn't coped very well. Even though she'd made love to Ty until well past one, it was barely a couple hours later when she'd woken struggling for air. For the second night in a row, she dreamed of the girl who had been strangled in the snow.

The dream hadn't been loud enough to wake Ty, but it had been vivid enough that she hadn't felt like risking another one. In lieu of sleeping, she studied her father's file in the spare bedroom. They were transforming the space into an office, and Ty had installed a killer computer. Unfortunately, even slick, high-powered electronics couldn't make sense of all the crap in her father's file.

"You're awake."

She swiveled around in the chair. Ty was walking toward her with a blanket in his hand.

"God, you scared me. I thought you were gone. What time is it?"

"Almost six." He draped the blanket across her shoulders and leaned down and kissed the top of her head. "I woke up and you were gone. I heard Beauty whining and carrying on, so I looked in here. You okay?"

She pulled the blanket tighter around her. "I am now. Thanks."

"Did you have a dream?"

She didn't want to get into the dream with him. "No, I just couldn't sleep. I kept thinking about my dad's file and how much I still don't know."

He leaned back against the desk and crossed his arms with a disapproving expression. "I'll be done with this case soon, babe. Why don't you wait until this murder investigation is over? We'll figure out what happened with your dad together."

She shrugged. "I'm on vacation until next week. Might as well use the time I have left."

For a moment he didn't respond. Finally, he said, "Don't get mad, but I don't think it's wise to look into this alone."

Annoyed, she leaned back in the big leather chair. "I solve most of my cases alone."

"Not the ones involving people you love. Trust me, I've been there. You *know* I've been there. Investigating Tara's murder almost ate me alive."

She preferred working solo. Always had. Being emotionally connected to a case only made her wish more strongly than ever that everyone would just back the hell off and stay out of her business. "I'm fine. You better get going."

He looked down at the desk that was littered with documents from her dad's file. "Give me a brief rundown of what you've found out so far."

She wasn't stupid. He was trying to judge how emotionally strung-out she was. But she couldn't deny that she wanted his take on things. "My dad was deep inside a drug cartel with another agent named Ben Steel. They were assigned to pick up a truckload of cocaine and move it across two states. The street value was almost a million."

She grabbed a report and handed it to Ty. According to the date, it was notes written by her father just hours before his death.

"There was no problem delivering the truck. Of course, my dad and Agent Steel had to inform the Feds and DEA of a shipment that huge. The truck was seized and a couple of high-up distributors were nabbed. Might have gotten a slap on the wrist, but I haven't gotten that far yet."

"Sounds like a test," Ty murmured while scanning the document. "Someone suspected they were cops. They were willing to sacrifice a large amount of drugs to pinpoint the narcs in their ring."

Ty's quick mind and wicked instincts appealed to Jordan in a way a great ass might appeal to another woman. There was something oh-so-sexy about a guy who could talk shop one minute and fuck you mindless the next.

He looked down at her. "What?"

She grinned and shook her head. "That was what I thought, too. It's easy to draw that line with the hindsight we have. We know that my dad and Agent Steel were both murdered within the following forty-eight hours. But they didn't see it coming."

Ty glanced at his watch. "It's six. I've got to roll." He laid the document down on the desk and tilted her chin up. "Let this be for now. Go back to bed and get some rest; you've been up all night." He smiled and touched his lips to hers. "It'd be very disappointing if you were too tired for a repeat performance of last night."

She rolled her eyes. The man was a walking hard-on. Every sexual area on her body ached from last night's sexcapades. "Even you couldn't manage a round two of last night."

"No?" he said, walking to the door. "I guess we'll see about that."

She watched his splendid backside walk away and tried not to think about the next several hours he would be spending side by side with Cherry-bomb.

On second thought, she'd find the strength for a round two if it killed her.

Ty parked his truck in front of the brick building that housed the Longdale Police Force. Surely today would have to be better than yesterday.

Longdale only had five cops and a chief. He knew every one of their cars. The car he parked next to wasn't one he recognized. It wasn't Isobel's, either. So already someone was there that he had no desire to see. Not at 6:47 in the morning.

He walked inside and down the small hallway to his office. A large man with graying hair and overalls sat in one of the rickety chairs in front of his desk. Ty was pretty sure he was Hailey King's father. Hailey's dad hadn't been home yesterday when he and Isobel had gone to the King residence to break the news, but he'd noticed the family pictures when they spoke with Hailey's mom.

Ty shut his office door behind him. "Good morning," he said.

The man's eyes were damn near swelled shut. Ty was pretty good at recognizing grief when he saw it. "You're Mr. King?"

The older man nodded, but didn't say anything.

"I'm terribly sorry for your loss, Mr. King." Ty walked to his chair and sat behind his desk. "I will do everything in my power—"

"Did you arrest him yet?"

Ty paused. He had a feeling he knew who King was talking about, but he decided to play dumb. "Arrest who, Mr. King?"

The big bear of a man leaned forward. "I don't have the energy or the patience for this. You know as well as I do that David Benson killed my daughter."

"Mr. King, we don't have the evidence that supports an arrest yet."

King's face flushed a furious red. "That's bull. You don't want to arrest David Benson because his father has more money than God. That's complete bullshit. We may not have a lot, Hailey may not have been rich, but Benson has to pay for what he did."

Ty moved around to the front of his desk and leaned against it. "Mr. King, I couldn't care less how much is in the Bensons' bank account. But I do care about evidence."

"David Benson followed her like a stalker for months. He was obsessed with my daughter. Her friend said they had a big fight the night she died. What else do you need?"

"I need solid proof. Some DNA, a witness, a fiber, something. We're being careful so that when we arrest someone, it'll stick. My job is to make sure I give the DA enough evidence to not only arrest, but to convict, as well. Sometimes that takes more than a day."

"But you're looking at Benson? Tell me you're looking at Benson."

"We're following all logical leads right now."

King sat quietly, appeared to do nothing more than study the tile on the floor before shaking his head. "That sounds like the answer you give when you've got nothing."

"It's the answer I give when I'm making sure I arrest the right person."

Hailey's dad dropped back in the chair. The lost look, the desperate slouch, made Ty's chest clench. He knew the role he needed to play, knew how important it was for Mr. King to believe someone cared enough to find the truth.

"Do you have children?" King asked.

Ty shook his head. "No. But I lost my younger sister to murder, so I've got a pretty good idea about how this kind of thing affects a family. Hailey matters to me, Mr. King. I wouldn't be here if she didn't."

King nodded and stood. Ty figured he demeanor it was more defeat than understanding. "You'll call me when you know something?"

"You have my word on it." Ty walked Mr. King down the hallway to the front office. Jonesy walked past them and said, "David Benson and his father are here to see you, Ty."

They rounded the corner. David Benson stood in the middle of the precinct's waiting area.

Ty watched Hailey's dad. Things were going to skyrocket from ugly to seriously fucked-up any second now.

Mr. King's expression turned feral and he lunged in David's direction. "I oughta kill you, you spoiled fucking bastard," King roared. "You think you're going to get away with this because you have money?"

Ty jumped in the middle, trying to head off the blowout, but King's big fist caught him square in the eye. "Knock it off," Ty managed as he grabbed King around the waist and hauled him backwards.

"Enough. One more step from either of you and I'll arrest you both." Isobel's voice came from behind Ty. He hadn't realized she was even there.

Jonesy flew around the corner, too. Just in time to help restrain Mr. King.

"Stop it. This won't help Hailey," Ty shouted over King's accusing voice. "Officer Jones, please escort Mr. King to his vehicle and see that he exits the lot."

Isobel pushed David and his father into an office on the opposite side of the room while Jonesy hauled Mr. King outside.

Ty stood in the empty room for a minute. His eye throbbed like a son of a bitch, but he didn't have time to look at it. He needed to tell Jonesy to follow Hailey's dad all the way home. Then he had to deal with the Bensons.

So he'd been wrong. Today was going to be every bit the cluster-fuck yesterday had been. And worse, he was still supposed to be on vacation. He may not have been the smartest guy on the planet, but he knew one thing for sure. The next time he had vacation time coming, he was spending it somewhere too damn far away to be called into work.

Jordan pulled into Ty's precinct on her way to St. Louis to let him know she wouldn't be back until late. Only one person could cut corners and produce a copy of Special Agent Ben Steel's FBI file with little or no red tape.

Bahan.

She also intended to stop by her own precinct. Even though she worked narcotics, she knew most of the homicide guys well enough to fish for a little information. Someone had to have caught a case about a young woman being murdered in the snow. This wasn't her first trip around the block as far as the dreams were concerned; before all was said and done, the murdered woman was going to connect with her somehow.

She could have called Ty, but instead she decided to pop in and scowl at Cherry-bomb again. Today she was prepared for battle. Her clothes were nicer, her hair was combed, and she wore a little make-up here and there. Not that she'd be posing on the cover of *Vogue* any time soon, but she knew how to highlight her assets when the situation called for it.

"You are a huge idiot." She chastised herself as she got out of the car and wiped her sweaty palms on her jeans. Caleb was sitting at the reception desk when she walked in.

He smiled when he saw her. "Someone looks awfully pretty today."

"Ty in his office?" she asked.

"Yep. Issy is fixing him up. We had a little excitement this morning."

The phone on the reception desk rang and Caleb snatched up the receiver.

Fixing him up? Her heartbeat ramped up a notch. Had he been hurt? And what did Isobel Riley have to do with it? If he'd been seriously wounded they'd have called an ambulance.

They'd have called her.

She went to Ty's office, filled half with urgency and half with dread over what the hell she'd find when she got there. From the hallway, she could see Ty and Isobel together, and the image stopped her like a good, old-fashioned sucker punch.

Ty was in his chair, and the redhead loomed over him, cradling his chin in one hand and holding something against his face with the other. Close. Personal. She couldn't hear what they were saying, but the redhead was smiling and murmuring to Ty.

The disastrous image felt like a train wreck she couldn't look away from. Not because there was anything wrong going on, but because the two of them looked so right. Jordan swallowed, almost gagged on how much sense the intimate little scene made.

Isobel Riley was attractive. Jordan imagined that most men might say beautiful. She was obviously smart enough to make it to detective. And anyone with eyes could see how Isobel looked at Ty.

How long before he looked back and saw what was missing in his life? A normal woman who wouldn't fear all the things he wanted most.

Satisfied that he wasn't seriously injured, she turned to leave. Isobel obviously had the situation under control. The ambition to fight for her man was replaced by a big wave of foolishness. And honestly, a little bit of fear that she just might not come out on top if Ty ever bothered to compare pros and cons.

"Jordan." Ty caught up to her as she rounded the corner into the reception area. "Hey, wait a minute. What are you doing here?"

She stopped, turned back to him, and noticed his eye was almost swollen shut. Moving a hand to his face, she turned his chin to get a better look. "What happened?"

He shook his head and rolled his eyes. "Long, stupid story."

No doubt, one the redhead knew every detail of. She pulled her hand back. "I need to go. I'm heading to St. Louis to check in at my precinct and talk to Bahan. I just wanted to let you know I'd be gone a while."

He stepped closer, rested his hands on her hips. "Didn't you forget something?"

"I don't think so." She kept her gaze focused on his chest, refusing to look him in the eye. "And if I did, I'm sure the redhead will cover it. She seems to enjoy taking care of you."

"We're not going there again, are we?" Aggravation was clear in his tone. "Are you mad because she got some ice for my eye?"

"Nope. Couldn't care less." She wriggled out of his hold and turned for the door.

"Jordan, stop." He caught up to her, stepped in her path, and cupped her cheeks in his hands. He leaned in and kissed her—long and slow and exceedingly intimate for being in the middle of his cop shop. "Thank you for stopping by," he whispered. "Please be careful on the back roads."

"So this is your better half these days?"

Both of them turned to the redhead. Normally Jordan would have been embarrassed that someone had witnessed such a heated kiss, but under the circumstances, the devil on her shoulder actually wanted to flip Isobel the bird.

Jordan looked back up at Ty. After a long, uncomfortable pause, she said, "Hi. Yes, I'm Jordan. Ty's girlfriend."

She channeled her inner ice bitch and held out her hand to the redhead.

Cherry-bomb barely returned the handshake before letting her gaze dip down to Jordan's boots and crawl back up again. Hard to miss the not-so-subtle sizing-up.

"I'm Detective Riley with MHP. Nice to meet you." Then Isobel looked up at Ty. "The Bensons and their attorney are here. We probably shouldn't keep them waiting any longer."

"Okay. I'll be right in."

Ty hooked a finger under Jordan's chin and tilted it up. The act always felt like such an intimate gesture. The fact that he did it in front of the other woman chipped away at a bit of the ugly uncertainty in her heart.

"Did you need anything else, baby?"

A breeze flittered through the air as Cherry-bomb whipped around and stalked away. Isobel's huffy exit was less than subtle.

"She still wants you. You know that, right?"

He shrugged and eyed her sweater and the cleavage inside it like it was a last meal. "And I want you. You know that, right?"

She smiled a little now, too. Because she did know it. And right or wrong, she felt just a little smug because of it.

"Officer McGee, my dad has another appointment. Would it be possible to start soon?"

Jordan looked toward the door of the interview room. A tall, thin guy with curly blond hair and big hazel eyes looked back at her. She pulled away from Ty. A wild shiver skipped down her backbone.

"I'm on my way, David." Ty said.

Isobel came from down the hall and stopped next to the young guy. "I think we're ready to start any moment now." She looked back at Ty. "McGee?"

"I need to go, babe," Ty said. "I'll give you a call. Okay?"

Jordan snapped her focus from the young man to Ty.

Isobel crossed the room and hovered next to them.

"Is that your suspect?" Jordan asked.

Ty shot a sideways glance at Isobel. "Depends on who you ask, but I really don't think so. Just someone we're talking with right now. Are you okay?"

"I'm fine." Jordan took hold of Ty's hand and squeezed. "That's the vic's boyfriend, isn't it?"

Ty nodded. "Yeah."

"Be very thorough with him," she said.

"Jordan, was it?" Cherry-bomb's face tightened when she interrupted. "We're not at liberty to discuss the facts of a case with a—"

"Actually"—Jordan unleashed a back-the-hell-up look on Cherry-bomb—"it's Detective Delany with the St. Louis County Police Department." She had a good six to eight inches on the redhead and wasn't above using it. "I'm not exactly a civilian. That is what you were going to say, isn't it?"

"Still, you are not a part of this investigation."

Jordan stood silent for a moment, incredulous. She hadn't wanted to bitch-slap someone so badly since the arraignment of the drug dealer who had almost killed her on the last case.

She held the redhead's gaze with a long glare. "You're absolutely right, detective. There are some lines that should *never* be crossed, aren't there?"

CHAPTER 8

Shit. Shit. Shit.

Jordan started her car and pounded on the steering wheel. For someone who was supposed to be psychic and intuitive, she certainly hadn't seen this runaway train coming. She never, ever, *ever* entertained the idea that the girl in her dream had been connected to a case Ty was working.

It wasn't supposed to be this way. It wasn't supposed to *work* this way.

"Damn it," she murmured, letting her head thud back against the headrest. There weren't any hard and fast rules about her dreams, but involving Ty in her visions any more than he already was didn't feel right. Using the dreams on her *own* cases was one thing, but influencing the outcome of another cop's investigation felt wrong. *Really wrong.*

What if she made a mistake? Wasn't she the one who'd spent twenty years hating her own father based on a mistake?

The line had to be drawn somewhere. Ty was a good cop; he'd figure his case out without her help. She glanced at her reflection in the rearview mirror as she backed out of her parking space. "Just once, couldn't you be less than a total disaster?"

In St. Louis, Jordan cruised along Market Street until she came to the FBI's field office. Thank God it was Sunday. Maybe she wouldn't have to play twenty questions with the geriatric bulldog who guarded Bahan's office.

When she found his outer office dark and empty, she breathed a sigh of relief.

Bahan glanced up at her when she opened his door and walked in. She waited patiently while he talked to someone on the phone and clacked away at his computer. When it seemed he might be a few minutes longer, she snatched a mint from his candy jar. He always had the soft ones that melted in your mouth like minty icing. He whizzed around in his big leather chair and started to work on a different computer, so she reached into the jar again and then stuffed a big handful of mints into her pocket.

He swung back around, hung up the phone, and shook a finger at her. "You owe me seven hundred and forty-two dollars."

"For what?"

"For all the damn mints you steal. Agnes rations me, you know. She won't let me have more than one jar a week."

Jordan grinned. "Where is super-troll today, anyway? I figured she slept under her desk so she wouldn't miss the opportunity to jump out and snarl at me."

"Please. She's a harmless old woman."

"Bullshit. She's like Yoda—little, shriveled, and seemingly harmless until you piss her off. Then she rains down on you like a shitstorm. And let's face it, she hates me. And I've never done a damn thing to her."

"She doesn't hate you. She just thinks you're . . . uppity."

"What the hell kind of word is *uppity*? What the fuck does that mean?"

Bahan pulled at his collar, looking uncomfortable and guilty.

"What?" she asked. "Did you say something about me to her? Are you the reason she hates me?"

"She, ah . . . well, she wanted to fix me up with her granddaughter."

Jordan sucked in a gasp and gagged on the mint. "Yuck. Is there a family resemblance?"

He laughed. "Kind of. Yeah."

"So what does your love life have to do with me?"

He didn't answer right away, so Jordan leveled a look at him like she had him in the hot seat.

"I might have given her the impression that I had feelings for you."

"What? Why the hell would you do that?"

"I didn't want her to hate me because I refused to date her granddaughter. So I told her I was hung up on someone else. She asked if it was you, and it seemed like a harmless fib."

Jordan leaned forward with her hands propped on his desk. "I cannot believe you did that. Now she's going to think we're in here fooling around every time I come by."

"No, she won't. I sort of implied that you shot me down and I'm heartbroken. Now she just feels sorry for me and brings me chocolate cake and homemade stew."

Disgusted, Jordan shook her head. "No wonder she thinks I'm a bitch. Why don't you get a new secretary?"

"Are you kidding? Agnes is golden. In under a minute, she can put her hands on any document I've worked on in the last ten years. Nobody fucks with me because they're scared to have to deal with her. *And* she brings me food."

Jordan narrowed her eyes and opened his candy jar. She stuffed another big handful of mints in her other pocket. "Say *nothing*. Men are assholes. All of you."

He chuckled. "That sounds ominous. Is there trouble in ranch-topia?"

"No," she said. But even she could hear the defensiveness in her tone. "I don't know. I don't think so. Ty's murder investigation has him working with a female detective from Highway Patrol."

Bahan stared at her. "And you think because he's living with you, he shouldn't be allowed to work with other females?"

"Well, smartass, the last time he worked with this particular female, he slept with her."

"Oh." Bahan leaned back in his big old chair.

"Seriously? That's the best you can come up with? *'Oh.'* " She shook her head and dropped down into a chair in front of his desk. "Fucking men."

He laughed. "Hey, just because McGee's in trouble doesn't mean I'm going down with him."

"I got news—you already went down with him. The exact moment you confessed I'm your Agnes beard." She sank deeper into the chair.

He raised a brow.

She hated that amused, you're-such-a-female look. It made him look like he should be saying, *Bond . . . James Bond.* "What?" she finally asked.

"You're really twisted up about this, aren't you?"

"No. And that's certainly not why I stopped by. I wanted your help with something else."

He held up his hand. "No, it's okay, I'll play Dr. Phil." He leaned forward and steepled his hands. "So how does it make you feel knowing Ty and this other woman . . . shared evidence?"

"You're a dick," Jordan said, but she laughed as she said it. "How do you think it makes me feel? I want to kick her ass."

"Does this woman have a name?"

"Cherry-bomb."

Now Bahan laughed. "Her name is Cherry-bomb?"

"To me it is."

She felt like an idiot. They were joking around, but the thought of Isobel Riley underneath Ty or on top of Ty or up against a wall with Ty made her heart feel like it could explode right out of her chest.

"All right," he said, much more seriously now. "I'm guessing you're overreacting as most females tend to do, but I'll give you the lowdown from a man's perspective."

He leaned his elbows on his desk. "First of all, do you *honestly* think he has feelings for this woman?"

She shrugged, but then shook her head. "Not really. I don't think so."

"How long was he with her? A couple weeks? A couple months?"

Ty would not be happy she was discussing this. Hell, *she* wasn't happy she was discussing it. But she did kind of want another guy's perspective. "He said, and I quote, 'it lasted about as long as it takes to brush your teeth and wasn't quite as enjoyable.'"

Bahan howled.

"I'm glad you think my life falling apart is funny."

He coughed and threw on his poker face. "Sorry. Was there alcohol involved?"

"I think so. He said that they had just wrapped up a case and went to a bar. Then they . . . you know . . . and then parted ways and never talked again."

Bahan rubbed a hand across his mouth as though fighting to hold back his amusement. "You've got nothing to worry about," he said.

"I know you're a good investigator, but you can't ask four questions and know whether or not . . ." She sighed, feeling incredibly foolish. "Never mind, you're right. I'm being stupid, and I shouldn't have mentioned it."

She dug into her bag and pulled out her dad's file to change the subject.

He slapped his hand down on top of the folder before she could open it. "Jordan, you *are* being stupid. How long did it take McGee to call after you had sex for the first time?"

Her mouth dropped open. She'd been to hell and back—a few times over—with Bahan. But her sex life with Ty was awkward to talk about. Plus she had crossed a lot of lines with Ty on the last case and wasn't overly anxious to admit that to Bahan.

"You don't have to answer," he said. "But my point is, I'm betting he cared enough to get a hold of you."

She nodded, remembering all too well. After the first time she had sex with Ty, he'd been waiting for her the next day in the parking lot of Buck's, insisting that they talk.

"I'm no expert, but in my experience there's a big difference between the woman you can't wait to see again and one you feel obligated to call and yet never do."

Bahan was right. Deep inside she knew that what she had with Ty was strong and meaningful. Overwhelmingly so most of the time. It was also complicated and scary as hell. "You're right." She nodded. "I know you're right."

"Of course. I'm always right. Now if McGee's working, you want to grab a beer? I can give you more pearly words of wisdom—Bahan-style—and we can talk about your dad's file."

"Actually, I have a few things about my dad's case that I want to research." She filled him in on what she had gotten through that morning. "Ty immediately reached the same conclusion I did. We think it makes a lot of sense that someone suspected my dad was a cop and that the delivery was a test. When the truck got seized, they figured my dad and Steele were the rats and murdered them."

"Sounds like a good assumption," Bahan said. "I'm glad you got some answers."

"Some answers, but not all of them. I'd like to see Steel's file so I can compare it with my dad's. And I still need to know who the Native American guy was."

Bahan rubbed his forehead. She was chasing a needle through a mountain of hay, and they both knew it. She wasn't sure how long his patience would last.

"Did you ever think that maybe you're wrong about this guy? Maybe he doesn't even exist."

"Or maybe he's still a part of the Delago organization. Maybe he's the one who ordered the hit on my family. I don't think I can put this to rest until I know who he was. What if he's still alive? What if he's still ordering hits on cops?"

Bahan's only answer was the shake of his head.

"If there's just the smallest chance I'm right, shouldn't we at least look? What if he does exist and is still out there? He could be running a huge operation of his own right now. With the databases you have access to, and both of us looking, we could scan through a lot guys with known drug ties in just a few hours. At least we can say we tried."

Bahan sighed, but she knew she had him.

"You're going to owe me a lot more than stolen-mint money."

She smiled and agreed. How could she argue the fact that she was racking up a hell of an IOU account with him? She was a little worried about the day he'd decide to cash it all in, but for now, she had a drug dealer to find.

Jordan made it home right about the time the sun was setting. Ty was kicked back on the couch with his legs propped up on the table, a beer in one hand and another empty bottle next to him.

"Hi." She dropped down on the table in front of him.

Based on the cool stare, he wasn't nearly as relaxed as he'd first appeared.

"I knew you were going into St. Louis, but I didn't realize you'd be gone this long. I tried to make it home so we could grab dinner."

"I figured you'd be tied up most of the day." She shrugged. "I had things to look into. But if you wanted me home earlier, you should have called."

"I did call. A few times."

He was good and aggravated. She reached into her bag and pulled out her phone. She'd dropped it inside her bag hours ago and never bothered to look at it again. "I forgot to charge it. Guess it died."

He leaned forward and propped his elbows on his knees. "Even if you're mad at me, it's childish to refuse to answer your phone."

"I'm not mad at you." At least she hadn't been.

"The tension today between you and Isobel was thick enough to slice. I could see how upset you were when you left the precinct. You're telling me the run-in with her had nothing to do with you refusing to answer my calls?"

"I didn't refuse to answer your calls." And he was wrong about why she upset earlier. It hadn't been Isobel. Not entirely. The tall, blond kid who'd murdered his girlfriend was what had thrown her. "I dropped the stupid phone in my bag and forgot about it. I'm not on duty, not even on call, so—"

"Being on duty doesn't have jack-shit to do with understanding that I worry. You drive like a New York cabbie on these back roads. Not to mention you're a drug cop, so every time you walk out that door there's a target on your back. The least you can do is answer your damn phone. I have always done that much for you."

Her temper diffused quickly. It always did when she realized his boxers were in a twist because he was worried about her. She never quite knew what to make of his concern. She hadn't had to check in with someone in, well . . . ever. But he was right. He did answer his phone and return calls right away. She was sure there would come a day when she'd be grateful for it.

"I'm sorry. I swear I didn't ignore your calls on purpose." She laid a hand on his leg. There was no denying the risks that went along with their lifestyle. "Really. I'm just not used to having to check in with someone."

He stood and walked into the kitchen. When he returned, he handed her a beer and sat in front of her. "Then pretty please, with sugar and a fucking cherry on top, get used to it. I don't like sitting here trying to figure out if you've decided to take on the wrong drug addict or if you're wrapped around a tree."

"I'm sorry," she whispered and pulled his face close to hers. With a gentle stroke of her tongue, she traced his bottom lip, tasting the tang of beer on him.

He set the beer down, clamped his hands around her waist, and tugged her onto his lap.

It was a weird fetish, she knew, but her fingers rubbed over and over the rough stubble on his cheeks while her tongue slipped deeper into his mouth. His end-of-the-day rough cheeks had a mystical power that made all her girls parts zing to life. There was just something so raw and masculine about the prickly sensation. And there was no doubt that she loved his mouth.

After a few minutes of connection, she tore her lips away, moved her head to his shoulder, and nuzzled into his neck. "So how was your day?"

"Well, up until about thirty seconds ago, it pretty well sucked. But it's getting better now."

She smiled and pressed soft kisses against his neck.

"Did you make progress on your dad's case?"

She let out a sarcastic laugh. "No. In fact, the harder I dig, the less sense anything makes. I'm beginning to think Bahan was right. I should have quit while I was blissfully ignorant."

He touched his lips to her forehead. "I can help, babe. I just need a day or two to wrap this up. We're pretty close to making an arrest."

"The boyfriend?" she asked.

"I guess. I'm not completely convinced, but Isobel seems to be. A team went through his bedroom and car today. They found a coat and a hat with blood on it in his trunk. I'm guessing its Hailey King's blood. Isobel thinks we have enough to make an arrest stick. And we probably do."

"How did he explain the coat and blood?"

"He says the coat was stolen weeks ago, and he has no idea about the blood. He says he walked outside the frat house after Hailey left, but got sick and started puking on the front lawn before he could follow her. Then he claims to have passed out. He doesn't remember anything after that."

"He's claiming memory loss? That's convenient," she said.

"Yeah, but I've got at least five different guys swearing they found him out cold and carried him back to the basement. Near as I can tell, we've got about fifteen minutes where we can't account for his whereabouts. I suppose it's physically possible he could have caught up to her, killed her, and returned, but something about the whole damn thing feels off to me. I don't think the kid has murder in him. I think he loved her."

Jordan swallowed back the guilt prodding at her and shifted on his lap until she could look him in the eye. How was she supposed to live with the fact she knew otherwise? "He wouldn't be the first guy to kill a woman he supposedly loved in an angry, drunken rage. It happens all the time."

"You sound like you've been talking to Isobel," he muttered.

"Ha, that'll be the day," she shot back. "But as bad as I hate to say it, she could be right. Passing out may *be* his whole defense. If he claims he has no memory, and you can't prove he was there, that's reasonable doubt for any lawyer worth his salt. You probably need to dig deeper. You can't give him a pass just because you think he's normally a good kid."

Ty eyed her. "What are you trying to say? You think I haven't explored every possible piece of evidence I can get my hands on?"

"I know you have," she said, backtracking. "But I also know what it's like to deal with guys who'd rather look you in the eye and lie than tell the truth. Even if the truth is handier."

Beauty sprang up from her blanket, baying like a true hound.

Ty's focus shifted to the dog. "She can bark? Huh."

"I know, right? It was a shock to me, too," Jordan said.

When Beauty barked again, Ty scooted Jordan off of his lap and headed to the front door.

"Someone here?" she asked.

"Looks like my parents. And Trevor, too. This ought to be good if my dad actually left the house."

Jordan got up and joined Ty in the foyer. When Ty opened the door, Beauty greeted everyone with a weird little noise that sounded more like she was attempting a conversation than barking.

Ty's mom reached down and petted the dog. "Is that right?" she asked the Beauty. Maggie laughed and looked up at Jordan. "You guys didn't mention you had a new family member."

"I guess we forgot, but yeah, that's Beauty."

Trevor chuckled. "I'd call her Franken-canine. Frank for short."

Jordan grinned, but she socked Trevor in the shoulder, anyway.

Ty's dad handed him a pie. "I know it's rude to just pop in, but your mom was dying to see the house."

"Hey, we're cops." Jordan snagged the pie from Ty. "You bring sweets or coffee, and the door is always open."

Ty kissed his mom's cheek. "Thank God I'm finally going to get something to eat around here. You could starve to death in this house."

Jordan accepted the jab as being well on target; she did suck at the domestic crap. But she shot Ty a dirty look for pointing out her shortcoming in front of his parents. "If you wanted someone who could cook, you should have moved in with Betty Crocker."

They spent the next hour showing Ty's family the house. Even Ty's dad seemed interested in their plans. After checking out the final closet, they managed to wrangle everyone back into the kitchen where they dove into the pie.

"Lemon meringue. Did Nana make this?"

It cracked Jordan up that a big guy like Ty still called his grandmother Nana.

"She did," Maggie answered. "She also made you a blueberry one, but Trevor got to it before you did."

"It didn't have anyone's name written on it," Trevor chimed in.

They sat around the table and chatted, but after pie and coffee, Ty shot Jordan a questioning glance. She knew exactly what he was thinking, because she'd been thinking it, too. Something was going on, only no one was stepping forward to say what that something was.

Finally, Trevor drummed his fingers on the table and said, "So . . ."

Everyone looked at him. Ty copied his drumming fingers.

"I've got a business proposition for you two. Kind of. You don't have to do anything really."

Ty leaned back in his chair and fold his arms. Jordan knew his mind was still on his murder case. That was the one thing people didn't always get about cop work, that it wasn't the kind of thing you could shut down and walk away from. He didn't look overly open to a business proposition at the moment.

"Dad is interested in cutting down the hours he puts in on the farm," Trevor said. "And I'm thinking about taking it over. That is, if you don't mind."

Ty looked confused, and Jordan certainly was.

"Why would I care if you want to take over the farm?" Ty asked.

Ty's dad leaned forward and entered the conversation. "Because your mom and I always thought we'd eventually sell the farm, the house and all the equipment and split it between the three of you kids." He blinked and looked down. "With Tara gone, half of everything is yours."

"That's it? You want to take over dad's farm?"

Trevor nodded.

"Christ, you looked so serious. I thought you were getting ready to tell us someone was dying or you were bankrupt, or something. The way you were looking at us scared the shit out of me." Ty blew out a big breath. "I think it's great you want to take over the farm."

"Well, there is a little more," Trevor said. "And I hope you guys will be up for it. I've wanted to get into the horse business for a while now. Like the Hendersons were at one time. Start slow. Breed for quality, not quantity."

Ty glanced at Jordan and then back at his brother.

"The other night you said you liked the idea of having a working farm but didn't know how you'd find the time to get the stables in shape or take care of the horses. If I used your stables, I could fix everything up, take care of the land, and keep it running better than it ever did. But I wouldn't have the overhead of building my own stable or buying my own land. We can work out the business end however you want, but we've both always loved horses. And we both know a lot about the business."

Ty looked at Jordan again. She shrugged.

"Don't look at me, I'm a cop. Everything I know about horses could fit on a fly's ass." *Shit.* Embarrassed that she'd forgotten to censor herself in front of Ty's parents, she snapped her gaze to Maggie's. "Sorry."

Trevor grinned. "If you guys work on getting the house back in shape and I fix up the stables, the property will be every bit as spectacular as it was when the Hendersons owned it. Hell, Ty, this place was built for breeding and training."

"Ah, well, I guess Jordan and I will need to talk about it."

Ty picked up her hand and laced his fingers with hers, but instead of looking at Ty, Jordan couldn't help but stare at Rick. For the first time since she'd met Ty's dad, he was smiling. And that, she figured, was reason enough for Ty to say yes.

Whether she liked it or not, she suspected horses—and Ty's family—were going to be part of her future.

Jordan made more coffee for herself and Maggie. "You might as well have another piece of pie, too. I'm not sure what's so fascinating out in that stable, but every time Ty goes out there it's hours before I see him again."

"Boys and their toys." Maggie laughed. "All three of them are just big, overgrown boys." She stirred cream into her coffee. "Thank you for not getting upset when Trevor brought up the idea of using your property and stables to breed his horses."

Jordan shrugged. "I may not be Sherlock Holmes, but I'd already figured out Ty was going to come up with some excuse to keep horses out there. At least this way he'll get his horse fix, but Trevor will be doing most of the day-to-day care. Seems like a win for both of them."

"It's also the first thing that's sparked any kind of response from their dad since . . . well, since Tara's been gone. He hasn't come right out and said anything, but I can tell he's thinking about how to help the boys get it all up and running. I can't tell you what that tiny little bit of enthusiasm means."

Jordan had noticed it, too. "Maybe this will be good for all of the guys, then. As long as I don't have to shovel any horse . . ." She glanced over at Maggie and censored her word choice this time. ". . . poop, I don't care what they do."

Ty's mom smiled and fidgeted with her coffee spoon again. Then she began twisting her wedding ring round and round her finger. Clearly, something was on Maggie's mind. Jordan found very few techniques as effective as silence to elicit information, so she sat quietly.

"I can't tell you how relieved I am that we figured out a way to keep the farm going without selling it. The thought of strangers living on our land or in our house is more than I can take. It's just a house, I know. But my kids grew up there. I have so many memories of the boys and Tara tied up in our home."

Maggie's gaze connected with Jordan's and hung on, as if she were clinging to a lifeline. "I realize I'm a crazy woman trying to hold on to something that's too precious to let go of, but so many things make me feel like . . . I don't know, I guess like . . ."

"Like Tara is still there." Jordan finished the sentence for Ty's mom, knowing full well everything between them was about to change.

Maggie nodded and her eyes filled with tears. "You blurted out Tara's name when you were at our house," she said. "And, well, it seemed like more than . . ."

"I felt her there, too." The words hadn't come easily, but they had come. Jordan knew about being desperate for even a little truth when everything around felt like a lie.

Maggie's breath sobbed out. "It's her home. I know that's why I feel her there."

"No." Jordan shook her head. "That's why you're conscious of feeling her there. It was a place you shared, so it's familiar to both of you. But the truth is, she'll be with you wherever you choose to go. Here, or Florida, or somewhere overseas, it doesn't matter. She won't ever leave you."

When Jordan stopped talking, Maggie's eyes went wide. The tears that she'd somehow managed to hold back finally spilled over and down her cheeks. "When you said her name, I knew something had happened. I knew I couldn't be the only one that felt her there. Rick says I'm crazy, but I'm not crazy, am I?"

No, Maggie wasn't crazy. In fact, Jordan decided the only crazy one in the kitchen was her, because she was considering telling Ty's mom the truth. "I work a lot of cases where violence and death are factors. I don't know why, I've never understood why, but sometimes I can feel the victims."

"Feel them?" Maggie repeated. "How?"

Damn it. She *knew* better than to cross this line. "Once they're gone, sometimes I have visions of what happened."

"Oh, God. Tara?" Maggie asked. "Did you have a vision of her?"

She'd come too far to back out now. Jordan nodded.

Maggie covered her face with her hands and cried.

What the hell had she been thinking? She'd traumatized Ty's mom. "Maggie, I'm so sorry. I shouldn't have said anything—"

"Yes, you should have." Maggie took Jordan's hand. "All I've ever wanted was the truth."

Then why did Jordan feel like such an ass? She got up and grabbed a tissue box.

"Thank you." Maggie plucked out several tissues. "For months I've been thinking that Rick was right, that maybe I *am* crazy. I just can't get past the feeling that Tara is trying to tell me something . . ."

Caught halfway between the living and the dead, Jordan would have given a year's salary to be able to rewind the last few minutes and start over.

"Are you a medium?" Maggie finally asked. "Like a psychic who can talk to the dead?"

"No, not exactly." Jordan balked at the label. She wasn't sure why; it was the most accurate term she could come up with. "It's just the cases I work. Sometimes I can't help seeing things. I mean . . ." What in the name of hell had made her go this far with Ty's mom? "I don't know what I mean." Embarrassed, Jordan dropped her head in her hands.

Maggie scooted her chair closer and touched Jordan's back. She sat that way for long enough that Jordan finally looked at her.

"When you lose a child, you find out quickly that nothing will ever be more painful. And even so, I've just never felt like she's gone. I went into her room and those damn pompoms ruffled. I didn't have the window open and there was no wind or breeze." Maggie wiped at her eyes. "And every time I walk by that swing of hers . . ."

"She wants you to know she's okay," Jordan said. "She wants *you* to be okay. And she doesn't want you to sell the farm." Jordan could hear Tara's words with stunning clarity. "The night of her death, she had been drugged, so she wasn't scared and she didn't suffer." Jordan knew that wasn't a hundred percent truthful. But it was exactly what Tara wanted her to say. She understood why, so she said it. "More than anything, she just wants you to know she loves you and that she'll always be here. Don't ever think she's gone or can't hear you just because you can't see her."

Maggie pulled Jordan into a hug. Not a simple thank-you hug, but a mother's hug.

It had been a long time, but Jordan still remembered the difference.

Part of her wanted to turn and run, but something stronger held her there. "I don't usually talk about this. Ever. I'm not sure why I did."

"Because I asked. Because I had to know. I don't talk about it either because the last time I did, Rick looked at me like I should be locked away in a mental facility."

Jordan smiled. That was a sentiment she could relate to. "Maybe we don't mention this to the guys. I'd like to stay out of the mental facility as long as possible, myself."

"Okay. But can I ask you one last question?"

Jordan nodded. "Anything."

"Did Tyler finally catch the man who killed Tara because of one of your visions?"

Jordan wasn't sure how to answer, so she gave the truth that she'd always believed. "I had a vision, and it may have speeded things along, but Ty would have gotten justice for Tara with or without me. That much I'm sure of."

CHAPTER 9

Three days later.

"Hey, wake up. Come on, baby."

Jordan vaguely registered a voice. Ty's voice, she thought.

"Wake up, Jordan."

She heard it again, but couldn't quite manage to wake. Then the soft brush of lips covered hers. Warm and teasing kisses trailed across her cheek and down her neck. She hoped Ty was the one kissing her, because she was enjoying the sensations entirely too much.

She managed to open her eyes. "Hi."

"Hi." He grinned. "You were having a dream."

"Yeah." She rolled to her side and slid an arm around his warm body. "I was dreaming about these incredible lips and all the wicked things I hoped they'd do to me. But you ruined it."

"Call me crazy, but based on the struggling and the groans, I don't think my lips were what you were dreaming about."

It was much too early to discuss a dream. She decided to distract him with a little playful teasing. "I never said it was *your* lips making me groan. You're not the only man in the world, you know."

Her words earned her a quick pinch on her butt.

"Ouch. You're mean."

"If another man's lips come anywhere near you, even in a dream, trust me, you haven't encountered my mean side yet."

"Maybe you should punish me then." She brushed her fingers down his chest, down his stomach, down the sexy trail of hair that led to the promised land. Then she wrapped her fingers around his warm, thick shaft. "You could remind me of just how thoroughly your lips own me."

He groaned. "I can't. It's after six, babe."

That was what his words said. But his body said he was thinking about sex. Seriously thinking about sex. She stroked him a couple times, and he hardened in her hand.

"You are just plain evil sometimes. I don't have time to make love—"

She let go of him and covered his mouth with a finger. "I didn't ask you to make love, I was merely offering you a chance to compete with the lips in my dream. But I'll just go back to sleep and fantasize about those *other* lips." She rolled over and away from him.

He yanked her hips back and nestled his erection into the seam of her ass.

She smiled. He was right where she wanted him—hard and pressing against her.

He slung a big arm around her and started toying with her nipple. His teeth closed on her earlobe, waking every nerve ending all the way down to her toes. When she shivered, he said, "So tell me, do those *other* lips make goose bumps spring up all over your body?"

The dull embers he'd stoked even before she opened her eyes were now a full-scale fire. He'd hardly touched her and already she was wet and needy and praying to God he didn't choose work over her.

"I'm not afraid of a little friendly competition if you need me to remind you how talented my lips are."

Yes, please! She could think of nothing that would make her happier.

He eased her back to the mattress and brought his lips down on one breast while he palmed and stroked the other. Her nipples hardened into aching, sensitive peaks. He'd vowed to make her come one day just from this, just from his mouth and hands toying with her breasts. She wouldn't have thought it possible, but right now the idea certainly wasn't out of the question.

His phone chimed with a text message. He rolled away from her long enough to grab the phone, but then dropped it on the bed and returned to her.

"Something important?" she managed.

"Not important enough."

His answer was evasive. She wondered if it had been Isobel.

But he moved his mouth to her other breast and she figured, fuck it, morning sex rocked. And she wasn't about to ruin it with ugly thoughts of the redhead. Thankfully, Ty had never walked away from a quick tumble when she offered it.

Of course he hadn't walked away from Isobel Riley when she offered herself, either.

That thought chilled her libido, as though a bucket of ice had been dumped over her head. She swatted his hand and rolled away. "Go on. Go to work. Stinkerbelle will be worried if you're late."

He grabbed her from behind and yanked her against his body again. Then he pulled her leg back and over his hip to gain better access. "Don't get pissy with me because Isobel entered your mind."

"Bite me," she said.

But even as she said it, his sneaky fingers slid between her legs and eased her open. He massaged small circles around her clit and said, "If you insist." His teeth came down on her neck. One finger speared into her, and after only a few thrusts, he added a second. The pad of his thumb stroked delicate pressure over sensitive nerves. She bowed helplessly against his hand.

"See, my lips aren't the only body part with talent." He stopped moving just to make her crazy. "I'll remind you on a daily basis if I need to."

He didn't need to remind her. She was all too aware that the damned man knew exactly how to shoot her to a fast, frantic orgasm. But he rarely did it. He usually preferred to draw things out, make her writhe and beg just a bit. Like right now. He had her body begging for release.

"Ty." She grabbed his hand in an attempt to get him moving again. But he slid his fingers out, adjusted her leg and ass, and pierced his entire length into her without missing a beat. Her breath rushed out.

"Christ. Okay," she gasped. "You made your point."

"Hardly." He grumbled the word against her ear. "I haven't even started to make my point yet."

He pulled all the way out of her and thrust back in. Damned if a bolt of pure pleasure didn't whip through every cell in her body.

"You teased me about dreaming of someone else's lips." He slid out, slammed back home again. "Then taunted me by wrapping your naughty little fingers around me. And just when things were getting good . . ."

Out.

Back in again.

". . . you tried to brush me off with a smartass comment about Isobel? I. Don't. Think. So."

And yes, each word was punctuated by a grinding thrust. She would have been furious if her body hadn't been singing the Hallelujah Chorus every damn time he slammed into her.

He pulled out, but instead of sliding back in, he got to his knees, rolled her to her stomach, then lifted her hips into the air.

She wound her hands in the sheets, anchoring herself for the force and intense pleasure she prayed was coming next. Ty never disappointed in the bedroom, but his playful roughness clawed at her with a sharp sense of anticipation.

No one but Ty could manage such wicked sex and make it feel so intimate and safe at the same time.

Her breath caught in confusion because he wrapped his hands around her hips but eased himself inside her. None of the quick, hard thrusts her body was aching for, just an easy, teasing glide.

"Tell me the truth, baby. Since you've been with me, have you ever dreamed about another man's lips?" He pushed in a little farther now. Gloriously deep, but painfully slow. "Think carefully."

She considered saying something to piss him off just to speed the pace, but thought better of it.

"No," she answered. And—*oh God*—was rewarded with several deep, hard thrusts.

He stopped, leaned over her, and slid a hand between the mattress and her breast to toy with her nipple again. "You're done with other men, aren't you?"

As he asked the question, he kissed a line across her spine.

"Yes," she cried out. "Yes, Ty. Yes. Please . . ."

His hands clamped around her hips again and he slammed into her with a force that scooted her whole body forward. She reached for the headboard and held tight. The feel of Ty's big body pounding into her again and again made her cry out his name. He stopped moving and pulled her back up against his chest. "You're all mine."

Unable to form meaningful words, she nodded and angled her head to absorb the full impact of his lips.

His tongue dipped in and out of her mouth. One hand moved between her legs, the other to her breast. His big body was all around her, teasing and tormenting as he drove into her from behind.

Nerves she never knew existed were trembling on a tightly strung wire of anticipation. She moaned—not his name or anything coherent this time, just a helpless whimper betraying the need to feel him everywhere.

Sweat slicked between them in heated streaks. His breath rushed across her neck in warm hitches. The simple morning tumble had taken a wild and delicious turn.

"Tell me you're done with other guys, and I'll make you come so hard you'll lose consciousness," he teased.

His phone rang. He'd dropped it next to them in the bed.

Jordan looked down. *Issy* was lit up in big glowing letters.

Seeing the cutesy nickname programed on his phone at the same time he was buried balls deep inside of her set her on fire. "It doesn't seem fair that I can't screw anyone else when you're spending all this time with a woman you banged."

It was a horrible, pissy thing to say, especially when Ty was still inside her and well on his way to delivering one of the most mind-bending orgasms she'd ever experienced. But *damn it*, why couldn't he see the truth about Isobel Riley?

Her head was having a hell of a time overruling her body, because as mad as she was, she still felt the clawing, desperate need for release.

But his phone rang again.

And again *Issy* lit up on the screen.

God *damn* it. The fucking redhead had radar that knew exactly how to blow up their most intimate moments. She twisted and jerked out of his hold.

But Ty had always had good reflexes. He caught her around the waist and tumbled her back on the bed. "What the hell's wrong with you?" He rolled on top of her and pinned her arms to the mattress. His forehead dropped against hers. "You damn well know I work with her and that's it. How many fucking ways do I have to say it?"

"Maybe you ought to try saying it to her, because she obviously doesn't get it. It's not even six thirty a.m., Ty. What the hell could be so important that she needs you at this hour?"

"I *am* in the middle of a homicide."

"Whatever. Then don't let me stand in the way." She jerked against his hold.

For a long angry moment, he glared like he wasn't going to budge. And from her position, she didn't stand a chance in hell of getting the upper hand.

But his phone chimed again. She knew it was Isobel again because instead of answering it, he picked it up and flung it against the wall.

It hit with a loud thud and crashed to the floor.

"Is that better? What else do you want me to do? Resign from this case? Quit my job, maybe? You let me know what it's going to take to make you happy."

"Instead of trashing your phone, why don't you try making an arrest and getting Isobel the hell out of town?" she spat back at him.

He sprang from the bed and threw on a pair of shorts. "Gee, why didn't I think of that? I'll just grab the first guy who comes along and arrest him. Who the hell cares about evidence, right?"

"How much fucking evidence do you need? David Benson all but admitted to it. Even your *girlfriend* thinks he's guilty."

"I swear to God, if you call her my *girlfriend* one more fucking time, I'm going to lose it. Seriously. Fucking. Lose it." He plowed his hands back through his hair. "It's a damn good thing David Benson isn't counting on you or Isobel to find the truth. Fucking irrational women."

"We may be women, and we may hate each other, but at least we both know the truth when it smacks us in the head."

"What's that supposed to mean? You know next to nothing about this case, so why the hell are you so certain . . ." Ty drug his hands through his hair again and closed his eyes. "Holy shit. You have *got* to be fucking kidding me. Tell me your dreams have not been about David Benson."

"They haven't." She snapped the words out. But Ty was furious and she had a sinking feeling that she was screwed. Her stomach twisted as dread clung to her insides.

Omitting the truth was one thing, but she couldn't outright lie to him. "They've been about a girl," she murmured. "Her name was Hailey."

Ty paced around in a circle, likely scoping out the next handy object to sling against the wall. After a few angry laps, he stopped. "I'm going to ask you this one time and one time only. You better tell me the truth. Did you see David Benson kill Hailey King in a dream?"

She swallowed. Hard. Then nodded. "Yes. But I didn't know it was your case at first."

"But you figured it out." He took a step back as the truth apparently started to fall into place for him. "And you figured it out Sunday when you saw David Benson in my office, didn't you?"

She nodded again.

"Three days you've known, and you haven't said a thing. How the hell could you do that?"

"Because . . ." She was unsure of the best way to defend her choice. "Because I've never let my dreams influence another cop's decisions. Especially decisions as important as arresting a suspect for murder. What if I'm wrong?"

"I am *not* just another cop to you." He was quiet and motionless for a long, miserable moment. Then he walked to the dresser, grabbed some clothes, and turned back toward her. "Or maybe I am. I guess I don't really know what the hell I am to you. You sure as shit don't seem to have a very high opinion of me."

"That is not true."

He came at her like a muscled wall of fury. "Isn't it? I've tried to show you a hundred different ways that I understand your dreams. Still, you hide everything. *Everything.* Even vital information in a murder case." He slapped a hand against his chest. "My murder case."

"I'm sorry. I just wanted . . ." What? She didn't have a good enough answer to justify lying to him. "To be normal, I guess."

"Normal? What the fuck does that mean? I got news for you, babe: there isn't one goddamned thing normal about either of us. My sister being murdered isn't normal. Your family being murdered isn't normal. Normal people don't dream about the dead, and you know what, I don't give a shit about normal. But I *won't* be lied to."

"I wasn't trying to lie. I'm just afraid the dreams are going to drive a wedge between us."

He let out a foul laugh. "Really? You think it's the dreams driving a wedge between us?" He stepped closer and pinned her with a vicious look. "From the moment you helped me solve Tara's murder, I have never been anything but fascinated by your dreams. I know they exist. I believe in them and I believe in you."

He backed up, putting several feet between them. "See, the problem here is not me believing in you, it's you believing in me. The fact that you don't have enough faith in me to share an important truth about a case I'm working on says quite a bit, don't you think? Then there's the fact you seem to think I'm stupid enough to fall back into bed with Isobel just because she's working in the same building. So don't use the dreams as an excuse. They aren't what's driving a wedge between us. I'd say you're doing a bang-up job of that all on your own."

Jordan watched through a window as Ty's truck peeled out of their drive. Not once since they'd been together had he failed to kiss her before leaving for work.

But he hadn't kissed her today.

In fact, he'd said nothing at all before slamming out the door. Even after a shower and getting dressed, he'd still been too furious to speak to her.

She hadn't bothered to make amends, either. Because after all, he'd been right about everything. So she'd hidden in the office fighting the guilt and pretending to study her father's case file.

She dropped back down in the office chair and frowned at Beauty. "What?"

Beauty cocked her head.

"I know, I know, I owe him an apology. But it's not like I can call or text him; his phone is broken."

Sitting in an unorganized room full of boxes and staring at a computer screen was only making her foul mood worse. Try as she might, she was unable to entice answers about her dad's case to magically appear in his file.

She needed answers about her family's murder. Real answers from someone who might remember what happened. After her fight with Ty, she felt just surly enough to confront the one asshole who might have those real answers.

Uncle Bill.

A few keystrokes later, Bill's address popped up: in a little suburb of Kansas City three hours away. She dressed, walked Beauty, and decided today was the day.

By noon, she'd made it to Bill's subdivision. As she was searching for the right street, her phone vibrated with a text from Bahan.

Can you come to my office? I have Ben Steel's file and there's something you need to see.

She replied: *How about tomorrow? I'm in Kansas City. Going to question my uncle. Stand by with bail money in case he's a prick. I don't think Ty will be bailing me out.*

He responded: *Keep your cool, hotshot. Call me when you get back!*

Bahan had given her the dubious nickname of *ice bitch* for her interrogation style. Since questioning a suspect was usually one of her strengths, he apparently understood that she might have trouble interviewing her uncle. As she rolled to a stop in front of Bill's house, she agreed that this interview wasn't going to be the same as those she held with strangers.

No stark white room. No big wide table. No other cop to play off of. And thanks to her fight with Ty, her emotions were already all over the place. Ice bitch was going to be a tricky persona to pull off today.

She studied the house. Uncle Bill had new digs. It was an average house, average yard, average suburb.

He was about to get a very *un*average visitor.

A car sat in the drive, and the front door was open behind a glass-front storm door. She walked up the little brick walkway and knocked on the glass.

He wouldn't recognize her. She was an adult. Her hair was longer, blonder. She was wearing sunglasses and make-up—a conscious effort to say: *look asshole, you kicked me when I was down, and I got up anyway.*

He walked toward the storm door and clicked open the lock. The son of a bitch just had to be handsome. Couldn't karma and time have at least turned him into an ugly troll?

She no longer had to wonder what her father would look like— nice build, salt and pepper hair, bright green eyes. Her dad would look much like his brother.

"Can I help you?" he asked.

Jordan took her sunglasses off and stared up at him.

He started to smile before shock widened his eyes. "Jordan," he murmured. For a moment, they both stood still, assessing each other in silence. "It's been twenty years. Come in." He opened the door and motioned her inside.

A small wave of relief ran through her when he didn't blatantly turn her away. It wouldn't have mattered—she'd have played as dirty as he wanted to play—but this way made it simpler. She glanced around the room, then turned to face him. "I didn't think you'd recognized me."

"Of course I recognize you. You look just like your momma." His brows knitted together. He took a handkerchief from his pocket and wiped his eyes. "Christ, I think you're even more beautiful than she was, if that's possible."

An unexpected jolt of anger flashed through her. She wanted to hurt him. Yet it made no sense, none whatsoever, for her to feel anything toward the man. He'd done nothing.

Maybe that was why her reaction to him was so out of whack. When she'd needed someone most, he'd done nothing.

But he hadn't been responsible for her family's fate. Still, the urge to forbid him to ever speak of her mother again roared in her head. Which was just fucking counterproductive because she had no intension of leaving until she'd wrung every last detail about her parents from his memory.

"I won't take up much of your time," she managed.

"No, it's fine," he said. "Let me call my office and tell them I'll be late. Would you like something to drink?"

"It's not a social call, Bill. I need about ten minutes' worth of answers from you. Once I get them, you can toss me out as cleanly as you did twenty years ago."

His gaze never wavered from hers. She saw the challenge. Saw that he wanted to say something, maybe defend his selfish actions. Instead he nodded. "Let me make that call. I'll be right back."

Jordan felt beads of nervous sweat trickle through her hairline. She knew how to do this. She'd made an art form of drawing someone in before turning them out so neatly that they never felt the fatal swing of the blade.

Yet in Bill's presence, she felt like the same hopeless, hateful ten-year-old she'd once been. The childish need to see him suffer was screwing with the trained cop.

She took a breath, flexed her fingers, and rolled her head left and right, loosening her shoulders. On the fireplace mantle was a picture of a young woman. Jordan moved closer, picked it up. It had to be her cousin Jessica. The big brown eyes were different, more mature, and yet just the same as she remembered them.

Her uncle returned, handed her a bottle of water, and pointed to the dining table.

In her precinct, she'd often choose to stand, take the point of power. In this case, since her legs weren't quite steady, she did as he instructed.

"What can I do for you, Jordan?" He eased down into a chair across from her.

"Are my parents and Katy buried in Saunders Cemetery in St. Louis?"

"Yes." He didn't pause or stumble with his answer, and for some reason that made the truth worse.

She reached for the water and choked down a swallow. "But you spread ashes with me. Were the ashes fake?"

"They were. I'm sorry."

She scrubbed her hands up and down her face, hopefully with enough pressure to hold everything back. She *knew* that question shouldn't have been the first one. She'd jumped track, screwed with the game plan.

Do not crumble. Not here. She forced her gaze back to his. "And what was the point of that cruelty?"

"The social workers said you needed closure, but we couldn't take you to their funeral, or . . ." He glanced away. "Or to *your* funeral."

They both sat quietly for a long, excruciating moment avoiding eye contact.

"Your father was involved with a very dangerous drug cartel."

"But he wasn't a drug dealer, as you let me believe."

"He wasn't. But his actions still led to what happened. Try to understand, Jordan—someone was supposed to kill all four of you. I did what I was told to do to protect you, protect the only member of my brother's family that survived. I'm sorry."

"You're sorry?" She echoed his words, managing little more than a whisper.

"Jordan, if anyone in that drug cartel had known you survived, you'd have been a target. Not a chance in hell a loose end of Jack Delany's would be allowed to walk around alive, child or not. They'd have never taken the chance that you could have heard something or testified against them."

He hunched forward, leaning into her space. "The only way to see that you stayed alive was by making sure, one hundred percent sure, the drug dealers targeting your family believed you were dead. I wanted to help you, but I had a wife and a six-year-old daughter."

"You turned me over to foster care. Do you have any idea what that was like?"

"I know you didn't understand then, but I know you're a cop now; you have to understand what kinds of choices I was facing."

She nodded because she did understand. There was no peace in his explanation, not for a young girl whose family had been murdered and whose closest relative had thrust her aside, but a little perspective was starting to break through. If she had a child with Ty, she had no doubt she'd go to any length to protect their family.

"It wasn't entirely about us." Bill swiped at the sweat beading on his upper lip. "Jordan, look, I know you hate me. I also knew this day would come. Please understand nothing was simple back then."

She glanced at his hands and noticed they were no steadier than hers.

"If you think I haven't felt like a bastard all these years, you're wrong. They were talking witness protection. To keep you in our lives, the FBI said we'd need to pack up the whole family and disappear. Allie was on chemo for breast cancer. I'm not sure you knew that." He looked up at her again. "We were a mess on our own before all hell broke loose with your family. I couldn't ask Allie to leave everyone. Not her mom or her friends when she was so sick. She needed her family. Hell, I needed them."

It had been easier believing he was a selfish prick. She really, *really* needed to hate him. Now she found herself sitting there without even the backbone of anger holding her together.

"I made a decision to take care of my family. Every single damn day I debate whether it was the right decision. But you were just so traumatized." He waved a hand aimlessly. "You had a mountain of issues, needed almost constant attention. You'd lash out, melt down, refuse to eat. There were nightmares—the psychologist called them night terrors—almost every night. The only thing keeping you going were the drugs that numbed you. With all that Allie was dealing with, I just couldn't . . . I'm sorry, honey, I just didn't know how to do it all."

Jordan swallowed hard. She'd been a mess, she knew that was true. "When I asked if my dad was a drug dealer, why didn't you tell me the truth? Couldn't you at least have given me that much?" she murmured.

He opened his water and took a long drink, then sighed like the weight of the world was pressing down on him. "Maybe I should have told you the truth, but the FBI has a division that takes care of family members when their loved ones are killed in the line, so I thought they knew what was best. Only your case was so unique that all of us—me, them—were just fumbling through it. I believed they were trying to do the best thing for you, and so was I. I did what the social workers and psychologist said to do."

"Lie to me?"

His expression turned harder. "Did you ever tell anyone that your parents and sister died because your father was a drug dealer?"

She shook her head. "Of course not. It was no one's business."

"Exactly. It shamed you, so you didn't speak of it. You were stubborn as hell. They tried to change your name and you refused. They wanted to cut your hair and you went crazy. We feared if you knew your dad was FBI and died in the line, you'd talk about it or ask questions."

"I'm thirty years old. It never occurred to you to find me and tell this information once I grew up?"

"What are you going to do with the information now?"

"What the hell do you think I'm going to do with it?" she lashed back. "I'm going to find the asshole who ordered the hit on my family."

"Yes, and then you're going to end up just like your father. The man who shot your family is dead. It's over, Jordan. Move on."

"I don't think so." Jordan slid the picture of Anton Linder out of the folder she'd carried in with her. "My dad's case file say's this is the guy who killed Mom, Dad, and Katy." She turned the picture around on the table and slid it toward her uncle.

Bill nodded. "Yeah, that's him. The neighbors heard gunshots and called the police. The cops chased him. He ran and jumped in a car. He was doing about ninety when he wrapped himself around a light pole a few miles from your house."

"It wasn't him. That's not who I saw do it." Jordan's hand had an ugly tremble in it as she grabbed the picture back.

Her uncle reached out, wrapped his larger, steadier fingers around hers. Until a few minutes ago, she'd have bet his touch would have spurred anger or an outburst. Maybe even hatred. Instead, she felt nothing more than the bone-deep sorrow that had just about eaten her alive over the years. Only this time, it wasn't her sorrow that pounded at her. It was Bill's.

"He's the one. He had the gun in the car. Your mom . . ."

"Just say it," Jordan lashed out. She yanked her hand away. "What?"

"Your mom apparently scratched him. His skin was under her nails." Bill nodded toward the picture of Anton Linder. "There was never any doubt that he was the one. But no matter how many times the police showed you mugshots and pictures, you kept insisting it was someone else. We never understood why."

"You weren't there. The police weren't there. I was there, and I saw a tall guy with long black hair and a scar."

"Did you really see him? Because you told the police you were hiding in a closet the whole time. And the man you just described couldn't have killed your family, Jordan. The man who fits that description was your father's partner, and he was already dead. The cartel had murdered him the night before."

"But . . ." The air in the small house turned thick and murky, as though she were inhaling through a dirty filter. She tried like hell to take in a few steadying breaths, but her chest felt crushed under the weight of the shock. It was nearly impossible to breathe, think, or talk. "But the other man, I've seen him over and over in my . . ."

. . . dreams. No, not going there.

"In my mind, I can still see him."

"Probably because he worked with your dad. You must have met him. You were just a child and under so much stress, no one blamed you for having the details mixed up."

Could she have had the details *that* mixed up? She thought back to the dream. She hadn't actually seen the man with the long black hair and the scar pull the trigger, but he'd been there. Always with a fierce expression and panicked movements. Had he been trying to warn her of what was coming instead of being the one who'd killed her family?

Closing her eyes, she thought back, tried to make sense of all the scrambled memories. Had she once again spent years hating the wrong man?

She stared at Bill and managed one last question. "Was his name Ben Steel?"

Her uncle blew out a long sigh. "God, Jordan. That was twenty years ago. I don't know if I remember all the names, but yeah, Steel sounds right, I think."

She cleared her throat. "Thank you for talking to me."

"Jordan, stay for a while. I can get you some coffee and we can call Jessica—"

She shook her head. "I have to get back." She was cool and professional now, so maybe he wouldn't guess that he'd ripped one more piece of earth right out from under her. She stood and headed for the door.

"Jordan," he said

She stopped.

"You're always welcome here. I hope you come back. I'd like to see you again. I think Jessie would like it, too."

She turned back to him. "How is Jessie?"

"Good. She graduated with a psychology degree, works with troubled kids." His proud smile was impossible to miss. "Seems to love it."

"What happened to Aunt Allie?"

"She died about four years after you're family died. The cancer just kept coming back."

So neither of them had had a particularly easy go of it. "I'm sorry." She reached into her pocket, pulled out a business card, and laid it on a small table near the door. She didn't know if they'd ever keep in touch like family, but she no longer wanted to blow up and sever the bridge to his knowledge about her father, either.

He'd provided more answers than anyone else had so far. Unfortunately, they just spurred more questions.

Ty managed to avoid Isobel most of the morning. He went back to the sorority house to speak with Hailey King's roommate again. He needed to be absolutely sure it was David Benson that Gena had seen lurking outside the sorority house the night of Hailey's death.

Gena still swore she saw David at the exact same time five other guys claim to have carried David back inside the frat house. But David Benson sure as shit hadn't been in two different places at the same time. Something about the whole damn case didn't sit right with Ty.

He pulled into the parking lot at the precinct, then made his way to his office to find Isobel behind his desk.

"About damn time you showed up," she said. "I've been trying to call you all morning."

"A fact I'm well aware of," he grumbled. He tossed the box to his new cellphone down on his desk. "My phone broke."

"Ah." She raised a brow. "And you never thought to call me with one of the other million phones in town? Is it just me who has this problem with you, or don't you bother to call anyone when you should?"

He worked hard to bite back a smartass response about blocking her number altogether. Jordan should know how committed he was to their relationship, but Isobel's ridiculous flirting and incessant phone calls were stopping now.

"Let me ask you something. What did you need at six this morning?"

She looked taken aback by his tone. "You know the coat we found in David's trunk? Labs show that it was Hailey's blood on it. The DA wants us to arrest David Benson."

"Damn. I can't believe that." Ty said. Then he cocked his head and looked at Isobel again. She was lying. He knew damn well she didn't have that info when she'd called before dawn. "Wow. They called you before six a.m. to tell you that?"

"No," she shot back. "I had a flat tire. I needed a lift. Jonesy gave me a ride. He's such a sweetheart. And," she added, "he answers his phone."

Ty sat in one of the chairs in front of his desk. He prayed to God she wouldn't use Jonesy as an excuse to hang around the precinct.

She leaned back in the chair. "Is there a problem?"

"Not at all." In fact, if they arrested Benson today, Isobel should be gone by tonight. He just wished he were positive Benson killed Hailey. "Do you think David Benson is stupid enough to kill his girlfriend and then stuff the coat he was wearing into his trunk?"

"Uh, yeah, I do. Maybe not if he's sober and thinking with a clear head. But I'm pretty sure he got angry and drunk, killed Hailey, and then barely managed to stumble back to the frat house before he passed out in the snow. The fact that he had the presence of mind to stuff the coat anywhere is impressive."

Isobel's scenario was plausible, he supposed. Still, his gut wasn't one hundred percent on board with the arrest. "I'm not sure I buy it."

"Hey, if you've got some other smoking gun in your back pocket, feel free to call the DA and hash it out. But I'm not looking in the other direction so that David Benson can strangle the next young woman who denies him sex."

Ty thought about Tara for a minute. And then thought about Hailey King's family. Maybe Isobel was right. If Benson killed another young woman because he got away with it the first time, that blood would be on Ty's hands. "All right," he said, "grab your coat. Let's go pick him up."

CHAPTER 10

Jordan made it back to Saunders Cemetery just before dark. The drive had given her enough time to sort through what her uncle had told her. Ben Steel was the man in her dream. And he hadn't murdered her parents and Katy, he'd been trying to save them.

All she had seen was his face and then the murders. She'd been too young, too inexperienced, and too hard-headed to figure out what the dream had really meant.

After a little digging, she found out that Ben Steel and his wife were also buried in Saunders Cemetery. They were several rows away from her family, but she needed to see his grave. Needed to apologize.

She placed a single red rose on Steel's headstone. "I'm sorry." It was perhaps the most inadequate apology ever. Unless she counted the one she was about to make to her father.

Turning from Steel's headstone, she thought about how a whole cemetery of truth had existed less than five minutes from where she worked every day. And yet she hadn't been a good enough cop, psychic, or daughter to figure it out. The guilt was like a living, breathing beast inside her.

She made her way over to her family and looked down at the four headstones, all that was left of a family who'd appeared almost normal at one time.

They'd gone to the movies. They'd camped. She remembered playing softball and eating ice cream, just normal stuff. Until one day, normal no longer existed.

Maybe Ty was right. Maybe normal never existed. And maybe chasing normal had been her biggest mistake of all.

She squeezed the stalks of flowers in her hand. Roses for her mom and dad. Colorful daises for Katy. Still unsure if having graves to visit was a blessing or a curse, she knelt and arranged the flowers carefully against the headstones.

Day after day, year after year, there'd been so many people and spirits and cases she'd opened herself up to. But the case that mattered most, she refused to see, like a vindictive child. How many times over the years had her father tried to connect with her? Time and again he'd tried to show her the truth, and she'd been too stubborn to pay attention.

"I'm so sorry, Daddy." Her chin quivered, and she clamped a hand over her mouth to quiet the sob. "Maybe I needed someone to blame," she whispered. "Someone to hate more than I hated myself."

The tears came in a rush. "Please don't hate me. Please don't . . ." She sucked in a ragged breath.

I've always loved you.
I loved you then.
I love you now.
And I've loved you every day in between.

Her eyes opened. She looked around. No one else was there. Correction: no person was there. But she recognized the sensation and the overwhelming heartache of her father's spirit trying to communicate. And this time, she let him.

So much anger, she realized. So much energy spent blocking all his attempts at communicating for so many years.

"I'm sorry, Daddy. I'm so stupid. I should have—"

You're anger kept you going. You believed exactly what I needed you to believe to survive. Now believe there's a reason you're still alive.

She sat quietly for a minute. "If there is, I don't know what that reason is."

Yes, you do. You've found the truth, now let it go. We're gone, but we aren't the only family you have. Find your family and then move on.

"Find my family?" She was playing the game, breaking all her rules and allowing free communication—no blocking and no resenting. So why did it all still feel so cryptic?

Let someone into your life.

"I have. I let Ty in."

Have you? Have you really? You and I are such similar creatures, Jordan. But don't make the same mistakes I did. Your mom would tell you it's incredibly hard to love someone so deeply and yet always be on the outside trying to get in.

While the sky faded to black, Jordan sat on the ground and thought about her father's words. Was that how her mom had felt? Always on the outside trying to get in and become a part of her father's life?

Is that what she was doing to Ty?

After a few deep breaths, she stood. Her father was right. Ty was too good a man to be stuck with someone who couldn't give him everything he deserved. He'd asked for the truth and he'd asked for her faith, and she'd given him neither.

Jordan looked down at her mom's grave. "I hope Mom forgave you. And I hope Ty forgives me."

Ty picked up his beer bottle and tapped it against Isobel's. "Here's to being completely wrong."

"You were just doing your job." Isobel took a long pull of her beer. "You still try to see the good in people. I've learned better." Isobel set her beer down and leaned back in the booth. "But you've been a bear all day. Seems to me you knew we needed to arrest David even before we got the call. Now I'm sitting here wondering why. When we left the station last night, you were certain he was innocent. I'm curious. What tipped the scales?"

He shrugged, wondering what Isobel would say if he told her that it was Jordan's dream that had swayed him. "I just kept going over the evidence last night. David being the killer was the only thing that made sense." Interesting to see how it felt to be on this side of the dreams. "It wasn't any one thing. I guess it was everything together. Opportunity. Motive. And I'm betting that if we'd gotten a blood alcohol around the time of the murder, we'd have been shocked he remembered as much as he did."

"Agreed," she said. "But we knew all that before your sudden change of heart. Even so, I thought you'd be happy, run home to your girlfriend. Instead you're in a bar with me. What gives?"

Ty scrubbed his hands up and down his face. Isobel wasn't too far off base. At this particular moment, he *was* miserable. Walking out the door without trying to make things right or kissing Jordan had made his chest feel wonky all day, like it wanted to cave in on itself. He knew the dreams were hard for her to talk about, but still, they had to learn to work this shit out because—

"Hello." Isobel waved a hand in front of him. "Still here. What's going on, Ty? My detective skills are telling me your attitude has more to do with your domestic bliss, or lack thereof, than the case we just closed. Am I wrong?"

Ty shook his head. "Jordan and I had a fight, but it was nothing."

She leaned forward with her elbows on the table, laid a hand on top of his, and gently squeezed. "Are you happy in this relationship, Ty? Because you've acted like a nervous wreck since I've been here. Did you ever think that the right relationship shouldn't be this hard?"

Fuck. Why the fuck had he come here? To set Isobel straight, that was why. "It's a bit more complicated."

"Maybe it shouldn't be." She brushed her calf against his and slid a seductive finger over the back of his hand. "Maybe you need some fun, a night to relax and loosen up. I seem to remember we do that pretty well together."

Ty pulled his hand away. "Issy, you're a great cop. And you're beautiful."

They were quiet, the sounds of clinking glasses and laughter growing loud around them.

"But?" Her playful expression had turned sober.

"But I'm not playing house with Jordan. I love her. I love everything about her. I have no interest in a life without her in it." And he certainly had no interest in any other woman. Especially not Issy.

There was heat in her expression now. "Then why do you look so miserable?"

"Probably because the first big case since the Titus bust has me teamed up with a woman I've slept with." He raked his hands through his hair. "Look, Jordan's had a rough time. Her family died when she was small, and she grew up in foster care. She's already had a lot of pain in her life. I'd never do anything to hurt her. I'm sorry."

"Don't be." She sighed. "I always knew you were one of the good guys. Guess I should have made my move quicker, huh?"

There was no possible way for this day to go farther downhill. He might as well just lay it all on the line. "After you and I were together, I should have called, but I didn't think it was a good idea to get involved. Still . . ."

She attempted a smile, held up a hand to cut him off. "I get it."

They sat for a minute in uncomfortable silence before Isobel cocked her head. "What's Jordan's last name?"

"Delany. Why?"

"You said her family was killed? How?"

Ty didn't think there was any real sympathy in the question; Isobel was fishing for information. The last thing he needed was for her to go poking around in Jordan's past. Jordan had managed to keep the murder of her family a secret for years, and it sure wasn't his secret to spill now. "A car wreck."

"Well, tell her I'm sorry. Walk me out to my car?" she asked.

"That's a good idea." *Thank God.* He threw some a few singles down on the table and followed her outside.

She turned and looked at him. "Will you promise me something? If it doesn't work out . . ."

"I'll give you a call."

They both knew it was a lie, but under the circumstances, it felt like a kind one.

Isobel put her arms around his neck and pulled his cheek close to her lips. "Good luck with your lady," she whispered before kissing him.

A car stopped behind Isobel's.

Ty glanced up, knowing—just fucking knowing—it would be Jordan's furious gaze he'd be meeting. He looked in her eyes and saw the flash of raw ache before the rage kicked in.

She revved the engine and spun the tires. Gravel and dust churned up like a storm blasting through the parking lot. What were the fucking odds Jordan would be passing by at that precise moment? Fate had to be a female. A female scorned by some dumbass man.

He pulled Isobel's arms away from his neck. "Issy, I'm sorry. I've got to go."

"Was that your girlfriend?"

"It was." *Was* being the operative word. Because he'd bet every last dime that Jordan wasn't rationally trying to figure out why she'd found him with a redhead pressed against him. A redhead he had a history with.

Hell, it sounded bad, even to him. And he knew nothing had happened.

Jordan's car was long gone by the time he made it to his truck. He maneuvered the back roads much faster than he knew was safe. The fact that he didn't catch up with her car told him she'd been driving way too fast. He held his breath on a few of the tighter curves, hoping he wouldn't find her wrapped around a tree on the other side.

Relief rolled through him when he turned into their drive and saw her car in front of the house. He blazed through the door, thoughts and explanations rambling through his head.

He found her in the bedroom closet, staring at her clothes.

"You got the wrong idea in that parking lot," he started. "We made an arrest in the case. You didn't answer your phone when I tried to call. Isobel asked me to grab a bite before she headed out."

The words were spewing fast and furious, as though a geyser of guilt had erupted deep in his belly. Maybe he should have stayed away from Isobel. He knew how Jordan felt about her, but he really had intended to set Isobel straight. And that was what he had done.

Jordan strode past him and back into the bedroom. Beauty followed her like a four-legged shadow.

"Come on, Jordan. Do you honestly think I took another woman to a bar tonight with the intention of cheating on you?"

She shook her head, didn't bother to make eye contact. "No, I don't think that. At first I did." She pulled on a jacket, zipped it up, then turned and graced him with a look. "But that was me being stupid, and you don't deserve that. I don't believe in much." She paused and swallowed and, he was pretty sure, she was choking back emotions. "But I believe in you. I'm not entirely sure what I saw, but you're not a cheater or a liar."

Strange how the compliment felt like the kiss of death. "And?"

"And nothing. I'm taking Beauty for a walk; she's been cooped up all day." The dog pranced, her tail flailing like a whip when Jordan grabbed the leash.

Completely at a loss, Ty could only watch as Jordan pulled on her shoes. He knew damn well things weren't fixed between them. "You don't want to talk about anything?"

She managed a laugh, or a sob—he wasn't sure which. "I can safely say that, no, I have no intention of talking about anything tonight."

"Okay, we don't have to talk." He moved behind her. As she bent to clip the leash on Beauty, he slid a hand across the small of her back.

"I'll go with you. It's supposed to storm, and I don't want you out there—"

She jerked upright and away from his hand. "I just . . . no," she said, tugging on the leash. She turned back to him when she reached the door. "I told you there'd be times I'd need to be alone. We'll be back in a while."

For several minutes he stood trying to figure out how a day that had started so crappy still managed to end up worse. Neither of them was particularly good at talking through their feelings. But then, they didn't have to be. The physical connection was enough.

So now he just needed to convince himself that Jordan hadn't recoiled from his touch like he was toxic.

Her phone chimed, and a new level of frustration ripped through him. Didn't the damn woman understand that you actually had to carry the phone for it to come in handy? Now he had no way of checking on her, and it was getting ready to storm. He walked over to the phone and picked it up.

Bahan had texted her: *How was it?*

Maybe it was wrong, but he didn't care. He texted back: *How was what?*

Her phone chimed again. *Kansas City? Your uncle? Was he a dickhead?*

Well, Jesus. She'd been to Kansas City and back? All the way to see her uncle and she didn't tell him? The last couple of days had been hell, but still she could have said something.

He texted Bahan: *Jordan is walking the dog. I'll have her call you.* When he touched her phone again, a picture of the last image she'd saved popped up on the screen. It looked like a picture of a headstone. He turned the phone sideways, expanded the picture. The headstone read: *Jack Edmund Delany.*

He swiped to the next picture. *Mary Elizabeth Delany.*

The next. *Kathleen Janet Delany*

Jordan hadn't mentioned a location where her family was buried. In fact, he thought she'd said they were cremated. He swiped again.

Jordan Miranda Delany.

June 30, 1983 – November 30, 1993.

His chest tightened with an unbearable pressure. What the hell kind of insanity was this? There was something damn unsettling about seeing the name of the woman you loved on a headstone. Maybe not so much the name as the date of death.

He closed his eyes and thought back. He wasn't crazy. When he'd asked her about her family, she said they'd been cremated.

He shook his head and wondered if Jordan *had* been born under some unlucky alignment of the stars. The world never seemed to stop screwing with her.

A loud clap of thunder shook their old house, and lightning flashed through the windows.

She could lock herself away in one of the extra rooms if that was what she wanted to do, but he'd be damned if he was going to stand here and worry while she strolled around in a storm. He grabbed a flashlight and jogged out to the stable for the four-wheeler. When it revved to life, he debated whether she'd have headed out to the road or to the lake.

The lake. She loved it there.

It was as dark as pitch, save for his headlight and the lightning breaking overhead. He knew she hadn't been in the frame of mind to think about taking an umbrella or a light. After driving the narrow path through the woods, he came out on the other side near a clearing. Her silhouette flashed into view when the sky lit up. As usual, she was perched on the giant boulder next to the water. Beauty was prancing around next to her. He motored up behind them and turned off the four-wheeler.

Now that he was here, he felt that maybe he shouldn't have come. He'd promised to give her space, but the storm that was brewing was more than just a little rain. Beauty raced up to him and nuzzled his leg.

Jordan didn't turn or acknowledge his presence, so he eased closer. "Still mad?"

"No."

She'd spoken—that was good. He crawled up on the rock and scooted behind her. After the way she'd jerked away in the bedroom, his heart raced. He wasn't sure he could take that again. He hesitated, then went ahead and wrapped his arms around her anyway. She didn't pull away, but she didn't relax against him as she usually did, either.

"Let's go inside. We've got maybe five minutes before the downpour."

"The rain won't kill me."

"No, but the lightning might." As if on cue, the thunder rumbled again, a long, low avalanche tumbling in the sky. He rubbed his hands up and down her arms. "It's cold out here. Come inside with me. Please."

They sat without speaking as the wind continued to kick up around them. He squeezed his arms tighter around her and kissed her neck.

She took a shuddering breath. "Isobel's the kind of woman I've always imagined you with."

His breath rushed out. Damn it. He *knew* they weren't done with that. "I'm not sure what you think you saw tonight. I swear to you, you've got no reason to be mad."

She shook her head. "That's just it I'm not mad. I wish it was anger." She scooted around to look at him. "I have no idea what it is. When I picture what's right for your life, I can see you with her. Probably why I hated her from the beginning. But I can see you married to that spunky little redhead and having all these . . ." Her lip quivered and she looked away. ". . . redheaded babies and living on this ranch with your horses."

He raised a hand to brush her hair back. "You're being ridiculous."

"Am I?" she shot back. "Because I bet she'd know how to cook. And meet your family like a normal person. Maybe even make a Thanksgiving dinner without a truckload of baggage."

The thunder boomed and the lightning crackled. And Ty saw the doubt in her eyes.

"She'd decorate with just the right furniture. And paint with all the right colors and put stupid little doilies on the tables. It would be pretty and perfect." She closed her eyes, but opened them when thunder struck again. "Then I try to put myself in that picture and I just never fit. Why can't I ever see myself in your picture?"

Tears streaked down her face, and he tugged on her legs until she faced him completely.

"You can't see it," he said, taking her hands in his, "because you've got the wrong picture in your head. God knows why, but I seem to be fascinated by difficult blondes."

The storm was closing in, the humid scent of rain was thick in the cool air. But if here is where she wanted to do this, here it would be.

"As to the kid thing, after everything you and I have been through, bringing a child into this world would be something I'd have to think long and hard about. The thought of a whole tribe of babies makes me want to puke all over your big pretty rock here."

Her gaze connected with his, and her breath sobbed out. He cupped her face in his hands.

"And since I don't even know what a doily is, I suspect I'm not going to miss having one in my house. Look at me, please," he ordered when her head tilted down.

The first cold pings of rain began to whip through the air and lightning flashed overhead.

"I can't force you to want the same things I do. But the picture in my head, the one that keeps me going and gives me a reason to get up in the morning, it's just you and me. I don't care about anything else. What you just described, it's not my picture. Not even close."

He touched his lips to hers and felt the familiar zing of connection. He knew damn well she felt it, too. "See, the woman in my picture has all these crazy dreams and sharp outside edges, but her inside is pretty extraordinary."

The wind kicked up around them and the rain fell in earnest. Jordan crawled onto his lap and wrapped her arms and legs around him.

"You're not stupid." He squeezed his arms around her tight. "What we have isn't something that you can *make* happen. I can't transfer my feelings just because another woman may have a little less baggage."

"A little less baggage?" She managed a sarcastic, insincere laugh. "I'm a fucking disaster on wheels. Do you have any idea what I've learned over the last couple of days?"

He nodded and continued to hold her tight. "I think so. Your father was FBI. There's a headstone with your name on it somewhere. And you went to Kansas City to visit an uncle you haven't spoken to in years."

It was dark, but he registered her shock when she pulled back. "How did you—"

"Doesn't matter." He kissed her cheek, her ear, her lips. Then he kissed her again and again and again because he didn't know how else to show this crazy, stubborn woman that she was all that mattered, had been all that mattered from the first moment he saw her. "All I want is you. For the rest of my life, I swear all I want is you."

"I want that too," she whispered against his cheek. "And some days I actually believe we can get there."

He stayed silent during the long pause and the shaky hitch of her breath.

"But some days I feel like I'm drowning in the past and that the right thing to do is to let you go before I take you down with me."

He grabbed her face in his hands. "Don't ever say that."

"I have to say it. I'm so tired of feeling damaged and guilty."

"Babe, you've done nothing to feel guilty about."

"Are you kidding? I blamed my dad all these years. I hated him. Talked about him like he was scum. And all along he was just doing the job. And I know I should be thankful that I'm alive—for God's sake, I'm the only one that survived that horrible night. But why? I still pray and beg to understand *why* I survived. After all these years, I still wish I'd never hidden in that closet. It wasn't fair for them to leave me behind."

She pulled his forehead against hers. "And, oh *God.* I'm so, *so* ashamed that you're trying to offer me a life, give me back a piece of what was taken years ago and I'm too damned screwed up to understand how to grab hold of it."

She sobbed, a terrible moan of raw truth.

"That's what I felt when I saw her with you—shame and guilt. Like the life you should be having was standing right in front of you, but you couldn't see it because of me. I feel like a virus that's going to infect you unless you move on."

"Stop it." He grabbed her shoulders, fought to restrain himself from shaking some damn sense into her. Through the wet and the wind and the dropping temperature, his blood pulsed with furious heat. "You're going to stop this and stop it now."

In the flashing light of the storm, her eyes were wide. She was shivering from the rain, but he had her attention. And *Christ*, he was just furious. And fucking terrified. Because Jordan coped by shutting people out. It was how she'd been coping her whole life.

"I know who you are when you're not lost in this. You're fierce and you're brave and you're determined. And I have never, *never*, seen you give up. Not when Warren Buck tried to kill you. Not when I needed answers to find my sister's killer. And sure as hell not now. Not when we're finally in a position to have everything, because that's not fair. Not to me. Certainly not to you."

He'd always known he wouldn't lose Jordan to the normal stresses—finances, work, infidelity. None of those pressures would be what tore them apart. But he feared the dark places that lived in her head almost as much as he feared the call saying she'd taken a bullet from one of the junkies she dealt with.

"Whether you like it or not, you *are* alive, you did survive, and you need to stop living like you're dead. Maybe you talk to the dead, maybe you see the dead, but you're not one of them. *They can't have you.*"

CHAPTER 11

Jordan fought the damp and the cold and watched Ty make quick work of stowing the four-wheeler and toweling off Beauty. He pulled Jordan upstairs and started moving around the bedroom in that quick, efficient way of his. He lit the kindling and added wood in the fireplace, then pulled their mattress from the bed and onto the floor in front of the fire.

He grabbed a couple of towels and came back to her. "You're freezing. Let's get you out of these wet clothes."

But it wasn't entirely the cold night that had her trembling. The man in front of her, peeling her soaked clothes away with such gentleness and care, had caused a huge lump to swell in her throat.

She wanted to tell him so many things. That no one had ever made her feel so loved. That no one else ever would. That his belief, his confidence in her was a gift she never quite knew what to do with, and quite honestly, probably didn't deserve.

But she was going to take it. For him, she was going to take everything he gave, and after all this time, try in earnest to move past the damaged little kid who had ruled her life all the way into adulthood.

She put her arms around his neck and murmured against his ear. "I'm sorry, Ty. I'm so sorry. You're right. I can do this. Just keep reminding me that as long as I have you, I can do anything." The heat of his body pressing against hers felt like a miracle. She kissed up the length of his neck. "I'm done with the past. I want it to go away. Make it go away like you always do."

He pulled her down on the mattress and covered them both with a blanket. He smoothed a hand up her waist and brushed his lips against her temple. "I wish I could make your past go away forever. I know I can't do that, but I can damn sure give you tonight."

Tears slid across her temples and onto the mattress. He was right. That was what they did for each other—eased the hurt. Made the pain go away. If not forever, at least while the breaking points were wearing thin.

"I don't want to feel anything but you inside me," she told him.

She kissed his chest, put her arms around him and pulled him on top of her. Oh *God*, that was what she needed. His weight, his lips, his hands doing all the things that took away her ability to do anything but feel.

"I love you," she said. "You're the only thing in this world that I care about."

He put a finger under her chin and smiled down at her. "You know the dog is going to be really pissed if she hears you say that."

She laughed and squeezed him tighter.

His mouth came down on hers as he traced a finger lightly between her breasts. He might as well have sliced her open. Her heart absolutely ached to make him understand he was handing her back a life she'd given up on. How could she possibly put words to all the ways he was changing her?

Her eyes burned and her throat tightened. Then he lowered his mouth to her breast and she groaned. A moment ago, she'd been shivering. Now heat was spreading through her chest, her limbs, her heart.

His teeth and tongue took turns lashing at her nipple.

"Ah, God. You're so damn good at that. Did someone pull you aside and give you lessons, or . . . *oh God*."

"Naturally gifted," he teased. "Haven't you figured that out by now?"

Hell yes, she'd figured it out. She'd also figured out Tyler McGee had a playbook. Some nights the only plan was scoring. Other nights he didn't consider it a win unless he wrung her out first. As he moved his mouth lower and lower—down her torso, across her belly—she was pretty sure which one of those nights tonight would be.

"Ahhh." She moaned when he pushed her legs open and pressed his tongue to her clit. No teasing kisses. No fooling around this time. Just his warm mouth surrounding her, his tongue stroking and lashing until she cried out, arching up off of the mattress.

Her core erupted in a violent tremble.

A wild growl tore from his lungs.

Fierce.

Raw.

Erotic.

She tugged at him, wanting to feel him slide inside her body while it was still trembling and needy. Yet he continued to move in his signature slow and tantalizing way, kissing everywhere, stopping at her hips, her stomach, even pausing at her breasts long enough to tease them to aching again.

Dragging her fingers up his back, she felt the sheen of sweat and the tight, knotted muscles. His big erection pressed hot and heavy between them. "Now, Ty. I want you now." She pulled his head close to hers and devoured his mouth, certain he'd enter her.

He took her lips as if his life depended on it, but when the big head of his cock pushed against her opening, he groaned and stilled.

"Fast," she whispered against his ear. "And hard," she added. "I want to feel you so damn deep I don't know where you end and I begin."

"Fuck, Jordan," he growled. "I'm trying to slow down, take it easy so I don't hurt you. But this day, this goddamned day. And when you say shit like that . . . Just give me a second."

His voice was pained. She knew what he wanted, knew exactly what they both needed—a physical release strong enough to purge all the ugliness of the day.

But it was a thorn in his masculine control when he couldn't hold the reins as tight as he intended. And she'd never understood why. If he only knew how damned hot it was to feel him wild and reckless, know that he was lost in her and unable to control himself.

"Time's up, cowboy. Now we do this my way." She pushed him to his back and climbed on top of him. "Don't treat me like I'm broken, damn it. Some nights slow and easy are fine." Barely restrained herself, she clawed his shoulders for support and lifted her hips just high enough to align his big head underneath her. "But not tonight."

She pierced herself and instantly felt some of the bitterness of the day fall away. She moved fast, treating him roughly and taking him hard.

Allowing him what she knew he wasn't allowing himself.

Soon he gave in to the rhythm. Each time her body lifted, strong fingers dug in and pulled her hips roughly back down. "Oh *God*," she moaned. Ty had oral sex down to a science; she'd never complain. But this, the big head of him blazing across nerves buried deep inside of her, was almost more than her body could take. She cried out again. "Don't stop. *Please* . . ."

He reared up to a sit, tugged on her shoulders, and sank his teeth into the curve of her neck. "Fuck," he wailed as his body poured into her.

His straining muscles, the hard length of him, the warm wetness filling her to bursting touched off a blinding, pulsing orgasm that shook her body and rocked her limbs.

Their chests heaved, one against the other. She ran her tongue along his lips and felt him in ways that didn't make sense. Physically he'd devastated her. Yet that was nothing compared to the scorching mark tonight had seared into her heart. Her arms stayed locked around his neck, with her desperate to stay that way as long as possible.

In the sated haze of being well-fucked by Tyler McGee, Jordan decided she was beginning to see the same picture of their future that he did. No matter what life threw at them, as long as they were together, nothing else mattered.

They'd been wrapped around each other, kissing, until Ty felt sweat roll down his back. "You warm yet?" he murmured against her ear.

"God, yes," Jordan said. She fell back onto the mattress.

"You don't have to call me God. You can just call me Ty if you want."

Jordan laughed, and it was the sweetest sound Ty had heard all night. And that was saying something, because the sounds and words she'd murmured while they were making love had been his undoing.

He stretched out next to her on the mattress.

She curled up with her head on his shoulder and snickered. "Apollo, Hades, Zeus, and Ty, god of rocking sex. *Oh*, that's what I want for Christmas, one of those statues of you naked, covered with only a fig leaf."

"Now, baby, you know it'd take at least a fig branch to cover me up."

She threw her head back with laughter, then she propped herself up on an elbow and wrapped her fingers around his dick. "I guess you are kind of giftedly hung."

"That's what I'm saying. I don't think it'd be right to make the other gods feel bad about themselves. You should probably just keep it up here." He tapped her temple.

She was smiling. And that was exactly what he'd hoped to accomplish. When they were alone, they always managed to get to a spot where everything else slipped away. He turned on his side to face her and brushed her hair behind her ear.

She was quiet for a moment, then she murmured, "My dad used to do that all the time."

He stilled, moved his hand away. "I'm sorry. I didn't know. Why didn't you say something? If it bothers you—"

"It doesn't bother me." She took his wrist and guided his hand back to her hair. "It makes me feel loved. Like I finally got something right by choosing you."

A tight burn spread through his chest. "I do love you. And if I could find a way to keep you locked up here, keep you tucked away from everything bad that's happened in your life, I'd do it. I swear I would."

She ran her fingers across the stubble on his cheek and pulled him close for a kiss. Afterward, her mouth stilled and her forehead settled against his for a long moment. Then she sat up. "You've done something a lot more important than keep me locked away from my past. You're helping me figure out how to live with it."

He sat up, too.

"I'm sorry for keeping the truth about David Benson from you. I'm sorry for giving you trouble about Isobel this week. And I'm sorry for getting so crazy earlier. I'm worried that after tonight you're going to think I'm not strong enough to face the hard stuff." She laced her fingers with his. "But whether we hit a snag in our relationship or some other part of my past rears its head, I think

I'm strong enough to face it." Her gaze locked on to his. "And I think I'm strong enough because of you."

Touched beyond words, he pulled her hand to his lips and kissed it.

"When my family was murdered, it took everything I had just to exist. The pain was so, so raw, you know?"

He nodded but had a feeling he didn't have a clue what she'd been through.

"Maybe that's okay for a while," she went on. "Maybe that's how you get through tragedy. But the thing is, I never moved on. I couldn't because I never trusted anyone. Not with all of it. Certainly not with the dream part. Then you steamrolled in and now . . ."

She wiped at the tears on her cheeks. "Anyway, I should have told you the truth about David. And I should have known Isobel wasn't a threat to what we have." She paused and then looked up at him. "Don't doubt that I can do this. I'm strong enough to get where I need to be if you just give me a chance."

He pulled her onto his lap. "I've never doubted your strength," he said. "I think about it all the time. Especially when I try to imagine a little girl hiding while the unthinkable happened to her family. I know I can't even come close to understanding what that was like. But you're not that little girl anymore. And you're not alone."

"I know." She kissed him. "I'm so lucky to have you."

"I think we both may have ended up lucky," he whispered. "And you know what else? We're both about to get even luckier."

Familiar with the sounds of Jordan dreaming, Ty opened his eyes when he heard a noise. He was disoriented; the bedroom didn't look or feel right. He blinked. They were still on the mattress in front of the fireplace. He felt for Jordan. The spot next to him was empty. He sat up.

Jordan had rolled off and lay on the cold wooden floor.

Beauty had curled next to her, trying to keep her warm. The dog whined, and Ty realized it had been Beauty and not Jordan he'd heard.

He laid a hand on Jordan's arm. Her skin was cold. "Babe." He rubbed his eyes, trying see a little better. It was still dark outside.

The only light was a faint glow from the fireplace embers and the small nightlight shining in from the bathroom. He could see just enough to know Jordan was asleep. And maybe dreaming.

Beauty turned her head toward him and whined again. A louder, more urgent sound this time.

"Jordan." He tried to keep his voice low and soothing, which was always in opposition to everything he felt when trying to figure out if she was dreaming or just asleep. The first time he'd seen her dream, he'd tried to shake her awake and then restrain her. She'd fought him. Hard. And then she'd been wildly unsettled when she woke.

Since then he tried to be gentle when waking her. Still, he hadn't found the right way to get the job done with a minimal amount of stress for both of them.

He smoothed his fingers up and down her forearm and realized just how cold her skin felt. Oddly cold. Eerily cold. He'd touched dead bodies that weren't as chilled. And if she were dreaming, she wasn't thrashing around like normal.

Maybe it wasn't a dream. Maybe she'd rolled off the mattress and gotten cold.

Beauty let out one yelping bark and stood.

He put one hand under Jordan's legs and one under her back and slid her onto the mattress. Then he covered her with the blanket they'd shared earlier. He even grabbed another one from the bed and threw that over her, too. But something still wasn't right. Jordan slept like a cyclone most nights, tossing and turning, even thrashing violently when a dream came. He'd never seen her like this, stone still. Hell, he couldn't even hear her breathe.

That realization had him panicking. He raced to the wall switch and flipped on the overhead light. Still she didn't move. "Jordan, wake up. Come on, right now." No movement.

Beauty barked again.

"Jordan, goddamn it, wake up." Was it just his imagination, or had her lips taken on a bluish tint? He yanked back the blanket and looked at her fingertips. Slightly blue. Scared beyond reason, he picked her up, tugged her limp, naked body into his lap and wrapped his arms around her.

"Jordan Delany, wake up. It's Ty. Come back, Jordan," he ordered, shaking her. Beauty started barking in earnest and turning in panicked circles on top of the mattress.

"I know you're dreaming, goddamn it. So wake up. You're scaring Beauty." Hands on her shoulders, he shook her hard enough to make her head jerk back. "Wake the fuck up," he hollered.

CHAPTER 12

Jordan heard a dog bark. And she heard Ty. Kind of. But her heart was still with the girl dying in the snow.

Hailey.

"Wake the fuck up."

The words bellowed like a foghorn. Her head snapped back and her eyes opened, but her vision was blurred as if she was just under the surface of a thin pool of water. And holy hell, her lungs hurt.

"Breathe, damn it! Breathe." A piercing bark and Ty's angry words penetrated the odd zone she was trapped in.

He'd strangled her. The tall blond kid with curly hair and pretty hazel eyes had strangled the college girl. Hailey.

"Take another breath. That's right, just keep breathing, baby." Ty pulled her close, pressed his warm cheek against hers, and her eyes fell shut again.

Hailey had been crushed when the boy knocked her to the ground. She'd fought him, all the while trying to understand how the person she loved, her David, could hurt her so badly. She'd peered into his eyes, scanned every part of his face. Then Hailey had stopped fighting. An odd sense of relief had washed over her.

And Jordan had no idea why.

"Open your eyes so I know you're okay," Ty murmured.

But it was Beauty's commanding bark that made Jordan's eyes spring open.

"Thank God," Ty grumbled. "Fucking Christ."

Beauty pounced on her stomach. If she hadn't taken a deep breath before, she did now, when the dog spring-boarded off her gut. Ty scooted her back on the mattress and dropped his head in his hands.

The loss of his warmth spurred a deep shiver. She longed to crawl back onto his lap, but he looked... She wasn't sure. Frustrated? Maybe even angry?"

"Are you okay?" she whispered.

"No, Jordan, I'm not *okay*." He sprang up off the mattress and stomped into the bathroom.

Beauty crawled next to her and nudged her arm. She curled around the dog. "I'm okay." She ran her nails up and down Beauty's belly. "You're such a good girl, aren't you?"

Jordan wanted to be curled around Ty. Didn't look like that was going to happen anytime soon. She wondered what watching one of her dreams was like.

Ty came back into the room, irritation evident in his every movement. "Why don't we put this mattress back up on the bed?" He helped her up and they lifted the mattress back on the box springs. His words were curt and much different from those of the warm Tyler McGee she had fallen asleep with.

"I'm sorry," she said. "Are you mad at me?"

He let out a long sigh. "Not mad. Disturbed maybe. But not mad."

"I can't help having them. I've tried to warn you—"

"I don't care that you had a dream. It was the *not breathing* part that threw me. Has that happened before?"

"Pretty much everything has happened before." She shrugged. "I've woken struggling to breathe, or lying in the floor. Once I woke up lying in the middle of shattered glass. I'd bought a cute little lamp for the nightstand, but it was made of crystal." She smiled. "Now I stick with the brass ones."

He ran his hands through his hair, then tilted his head back as if life's answers were scrolled across the ceiling. "Was it my case you were dreaming about?"

"Yes."

"Then you need to stop dreaming about it." He dropped down on the bed. "We arrested David Benson yesterday. It's over."

She sat next to him and bumped her shoulder against his. "I don't think so. If I'm still dreaming about Hailey and David, there's a reason for it. Why don't you get ready for work and I'll try to sort through this."

He put an arm around her shoulders and pulled her in for a kiss. "I'm sorry for getting upset. I'm exactly where I need to be." He kissed her again and then asked, "What did you mean that you'd sort through it? How do you do that?"

She shrugged. "I'll journal it, try to get down as many details as I can."

"You have a dream journal?" The shock in his tone said it was just one more thing she'd failed to share. "Where?"

She nodded at the nightstand at her side of the bed.

He went to it and opened the drawer. After fishing around for a second, he pulled out a beat-up spiral notebook. "Is this it?"

She nodded.

"Okay, then. Let's do this."

Ty let Beauty outside and made coffee. He grabbed some cookies and headed back to the bedroom. By the time he crawled under the covers next to Jordan, she was dozing again. He kissed her forehead "Wake up, sleepyhead. I brought you coffee and breakfast in bed."

She sat up, scooted back against the headboard, and eyed the package of Oreos he'd tossed on the comforter. "When I brought you breakfast in bed, there were eggs and bacon."

He adjusted a couple pillows and leaned back. "Don't be jealous because I make a better breakfast than you. Oreos should be a required food group—you know it, and I know it. The world needs to stop with all this protein crap."

"Ah, yes." She smiled. "Who needs nutrients, anyway?"

"Exactly. Eat your cookie, then we'll do this." He picked up her journal. "May I?"

She shrugged. "You probably won't be able to read most of it. My handwriting isn't great after a dream. It's just notes, nothing that will make sense to anyone but me."

"Maybe not. Still, I'd like to see it."

After a moment, she nodded.

He opened the notebook and flipped through the pages, studying the dates and information. "This is incredible." He looked over at her. "How many cases do you think you've solved?"

"I don't know, and I'm not sure how much to attribute to being a good investigator and how much is because of the dreams. Either way, I've got a pretty good track record." She grabbed a cookie and twisted it apart. "I was the second-youngest person to make detective in my precinct. The youngest female. That pissed off more than a few guys."

"I bet." Ty grinned and turned to a blank page. "You know, you could tell me about the dream and I could write for you."

She glanced at the journal and swallowed down a bite of cookie.

Usually Ty was pretty good at sensing her moods, but her silence made him worry that he'd overstepped or treaded on sacred ground. "I don't have to. I mean I was just offering."

"No, that would actually be good." She picked up the pen and handed it to him. "Start with the date and time of the dream, just like you would when you're talking to a witness. If I don't know who the victim is, or where the crime happened, I jot down a little of the surroundings, time of day, temperature, anything that might shed light. Since you already have that info, we'll skip it."

He watched as Jordan closed her eyes and took a couple of deep breaths.

"It was unbearably cold," she started. "The ground was covered in snow. I don't know what time it was. No one else was around, so I'm guessing it was late. Like really late, after everyone else is already where they're going to crash for the night."

Jordan tossed down the cookie and went on. "She was trying to get home, and I wasn't sure why at first, but she stopped and looked around. She looked down the street, debating, I think, then she decided to cut through some kind of a park or field, or something like that."

The ravine. Ty knew exactly what Jordan was describing.

"She was about halfway through this field thing when she heard sounds, like footsteps crunching in the snow behind her. When she turned, there was nothing. She started walking and heard the sound again, only this time she figured it was coming from the cluster of trees to her right. She picked up the pace, had almost started to run, when he called her name."

Watching Jordan recall the vision was remarkable. It was like skipping to the end of a book before the whole mystery had unfolded.

No, it was like watching a playback of the mystery *as* it unfolded.

She opened her eyes and looked down at the journal. "Um, cowboy? In order to log this dream, you need to actually write down the details."

"Shit. Sorry." The only thing on the page was the date and time. "I was just watching and . . . It's like you go somewhere else when you do that. I can't decide if it's the coolest thing I've ever seen or completely terrifying."

"Yeah." She laughed. "I've debated the same thing myself." She took the pen out of his hand, then grabbed the journal. "I've got this. I've done it many times before."

"I can help, I swear I can."

Jordan held up a hand to quiet him and closed her eyes again.

"Hailey turned around, and the thing is, she was relieved to see him. She even said his name. Then she hurried to him and hugged him. The weird thing was, she pulled back right away. I think it may have been the smell."

Jordan opened her eyes, but still seemed focused on the memory. "I remember feeling my nose burn and clog, which is usually a sign that a victim is trying to make me aware of an unusual odor. And he didn't return her hug back, which bothered her, too, I think."

Ty watched Jordan scribble down thoughts and impressions without even looking at the paper:

She said his name—David
Abnormal smell
No response from the hug

Impressed that she could home in on the dream and still write, Ty didn't try to take back the job. She ran through the next few events, talking and sporadically writing. Her breathing became labored when she recapped Hailey struggling with David.

"But when he grabbed her hair, she knew."

Jordan's hand became increasingly unsteady. Ty eased the pen and pad out of her hands and began to write.

"With quick, violent deaths, most people never come to the realization they're about to die," she said. "Even as their car is spinning out or they're looking down the barrel of a gun, their mind is always working on how to fix the situation. But once he hit her and fell on top of her, Hailey knew she wasn't walking away. Still, I can't help feeling that she was fighting more to understand what was happening than she was to escape."

Jordan wasn't asleep, her eyes were open, and she was talking while analyzing the dream. But if Ty were a betting man, Jordan wasn't seeing him, their bedroom, or the damn dog that had jumped up on the foot of the bed. If he had to lay money on it, he suspected Jordan was more in Hailey's world than his right now.

"He hit her across the cheek and there was rage in his face—so much rage—and still she just kept asking over and over, 'what have I done?' and 'what happened?' When he put his hands around her throat and leaned in to choke her, getting as close as lovers do, it was like a switch flipped inside her. All at once something made sense and she stopped fighting, as though she'd instantly made peace with what was happening." Jordan turned and focused on Ty. "And that reaction is driving me nuts because it makes absolutely no sense at all. What the hell did she see?"

Ty felt his pulse hammering away, and again he'd failed to write a lot of what she'd said. Now she was staring at him as if he might have something to add. But after she'd shared this incredible thing she could do, he had no clue what to say.

"I'm sorry, Ty. I know a part of you still thinks he's innocent. I don't know why he did it, but he did."

Ty nodded. Every piece of evidence pointed to David Benson. Now Jordan's dream confirmed that he was the killer. "So much for my instincts, I guess."

Jordan picked up his hand and laced her fingers with his. "We're not perfect, Ty. Just because we're cops, that doesn't mean we have all the answers. Not even me, and I've often got more insight than other cops. Still, I don't always get things right."

"Are they ever wrong? The dreams, I mean. Because the ones you've told me about have been very accurate."

She sat up straighter, tilted her head as if deep in thought. "The dreams are never wrong, but sometimes I am."

"Jordan . . ." He tapped her cheek and turned her face toward his. "What is it?"

She told him about Ben Steele. About believing that he'd been the killer when in truth he'd been determined to save his partner's family.

"I feel like an idiot. I've had dream after dream where my mother and father would appear—Ben Steele, too—and every single time I'd shut it down. Kick, scream, do anything possible to wrestle myself awake. I was arrogant, thought I had it all figured out, and I was so wrong."

He pulled her against him. "You just told me to cut myself some slack, that we're not perfect. It may have taken more time than you wanted, but you're figuring out what happened to your dad."

"Am I? Because I feel like there's still a lot I don't know. How far was he inside the Delago organization? What did he know that cost so many lives? Why not just kill him and Steele? Why execute their families too?"

"It was a long time ago, baby. You may never get those answers. If you let me wrap Hailey King's murder up, I'll do anything you need to help figure out as much as we can."

Jordan turned her head and smiled up at him. "I'm going to marry you some day."

Ty's mouth dropped open. He knew he needed to say something. "Are you proposing to me?"

She sat up, crossed her legs, and propped her elbows on her knees as if preparing to calmly discuss the weather. "No way, cowboy. I've been screwed out of way too many good family memories. No way I'm getting screwed out of the memory of you proposing."

He sat up straighter, too, trying to figure out what had sparked such an un-Jordan-like comment. "Baby, if you want to get married, just—"

She held up a hand. "I'm not saying that, and I'm not even asking you to propose. It's just that it occurred to me that I've given you trouble around every turn, and you might be afraid to bring up the subject." She shrugged. "I wanted you to know, if you can still be here after seeing the dreams, after knowing what a screwed up life I've led, even writing in my journal for crap's sake, well, it may be the first time in my life I have ever seen a future, but I can see one with you."

He smiled. "So this proposal, you wouldn't want it to be a spur of the moment thing while we're eating Oreos in bed and journaling a murder, I take it?"

She smiled back. "At the risk of sounding like a bitch, I think you can do better." She gave him a quick peck on the lips. "Now let's get back to business."

Fairly certain he *could* do better, he let her drop the issue. For now. Although she *had* opened a door and he had every intention of walking through it before she changed her mind. He tossed the cookies on the nightstand and shooed Beauty off the bed. Tackling Jordan, he pinned her under his body with her arms above her head.

"You're right, we have unfinished business. Where were we?" He kissed her neck and her ear.

"Discussing a case, I think."

"Weren't we done with that?" He planted a slow, deep kiss against her lips.

"No, I don't think we were." She murmured and stretched up to check the clock. "Plus, I promised Bahan I'd go to his office first thing this morning."

"You're on vacation. Maybe we could spend an hour or two—"

"Ty." She pushed him off and sat up. "What are you going to do about David Benson?"

Christ. What *was* he going to do? He'd like to think he'd solved a murder, so why the hell didn't it feel that way? He slung an arm over his eyes. "A shitload of paperwork, I guess."

"Ty." She tugged his arm away and looked down at him. "Honestly, what do your instincts tell you about David?"

"I don't know, Jordan. I guess the kid fooled me, because even when we went to arrest him, I still couldn't wrap my head around his guilt. It's like it's too easy. If he's a clever sociopath who killed his girlfriend and can lie so convincingly through his teeth, why the hell would he toss a bloodstained coat in his trunk? Doesn't add up."

"Yeah," she agreed. "I'd think just about everybody would know to get rid of the evidence. So could someone be setting David up?"

He looked at her. "That's not what your dream showed."

"I just explained that I don't always know what my dreams are showing at first. I still think Hailey is trying to tell me something that I'm just not getting. And I know you have doubts about

David's guilt. How hard would it be to get me inside to talk to David tonight?"

"Ha," he said. "Not happening. Once his dad and lawyer entered the mix, I hardly got to talk to him. Although I'd love to see what kind of feel you get from David."

Ty watched her slide her sleek, naked body out of bed and gather up underclothes from the dresser. The woman was long, lean, and lethal. *Damn.* He glanced at the clock, too.

"Where is he now?" she asked.

"Huh? Who?"

Jordan rolled her eyes. "Your suspect. The guy we've been talking about all morning."

"In a holding cell in Cooper." Ty got up, too, decided to convince Jordan to at least conserve water. "You taking a shower?"

"Yes. Alone." She pushed him back down on the bed with one finger. "You have friends in Cooper? Someone who could get us in to see David tonight?"

"I think it's our job as concerned citizens and officers of the law to conserve water once in a while."

"Not happening. I told you, I'm meeting Bahan this morning."

"You don't have a time schedule, do you?"

"Tyler, focus please. Up here." She pointed to her face. "Do you know anyone who can get us in tonight?"

"I know all the guys in Cooper. Getting in to see him isn't the problem, but his dad and lawyer will fry me if we attempt to talk to him." He stood again and stalked in her direction as she backed toward the bathroom.

"Not if David agrees to it. He's a legal adult, right?"

Ty stopped. "Why on earth would he do that?"

"Because I can be very persuasive. And you're not the only one with wicked instincts. He may get past one of us, but he's going to need to be a damn good liar to fool us both. And if he's innocent, he'll want the truth as badly as we do. Now go find something to do while I shower. Alone." She took one step back and slammed the door.

Ty grinned. The last time he checked, their bathroom door didn't have a lock on it.

CHAPTER 13

Jordan and Ty sat in the lobby of the Cooper Municipal Building, waiting to be escorted back to the holding cells to talk with David Benson.

"This place is pretty nice. And about twenty times bigger than Longdale. You should try to get hired on here. Maybe the pay and benefits are better."

Ty let out a sarcastic laugh. "I wasn't kidding about the politics in small towns and in small-town police departments. I like it just fine where I am. Besides, Chief Donner will probably retire in the next couple of years. Good chance I'll be police chief before I'm thirty-five."

"Really?" Jordan smoothed her hand up his thigh. "Chief McGee," she whispered in his ear. "That sounds powerful and sexy. Kind of turns me on." She fell into her best Scarlett O'Hara imitation. "Oh no, Chief McGee. Don't lock me in that cell and do all those wicked, wicked things to my body again."

It didn't happen often, but she loved to see big, strong Tyler McGee turn three successive shades of red.

He grinned and shook his head. "Sounds like all the incentive I need to stay right where I am and become chief."

A few minutes later a uniformed cop approached them, made some small talk with Ty, and then led them back to David's cell.

"Since you're a narcotics specialist and have experience with suspects who claim to have blacked out, Chief Donner said you can consult on this case," Ty whispered as he dropped a small electronic device into her hand. "But remember to use the recorder. If you get him to waive his rights to an attorney, we want proof."

"This isn't my first rodeo, cowboy. Relax."

"You want me to go in with you?" he asked.

"Hell, no. You arrested him; right now you're the last person he wants to see. You need to stay far away if you want him to talk." She walked down the row of cells and stopped at the one David Benson was sitting in. "Hi, David."

He lifted his head, but didn't say anything.

"I'm Detective Jordan Delany from St. Louis. Officer McGee is a friend of mine. I'm also a narcotics specialist. Which means I've worked with people who've had lapses in memory from drugs or alcohol. I was wondering if maybe I could come in and talk to you."

"My dad said I can't talk to anyone without my lawyer," he muttered. His voice shook. With his big mop of blond curls and his wild eyes, the kid looked like a big, terrified, overgrown puppy. No wonder Ty had had such a hard time arresting him.

"You're right, you have every right to have a lawyer present. But I'm not here to try to get you to confess. I'm here to help find the truth, whatever that truth may be."

The kid still didn't answer, just looked down at the tile.

"You can go to the arraignment tomorrow morning and Officer McGee can present all the evidence against you. And most likely you'll be charged with murder. Or you can give me one chance to try to make sense of all this. And to figure out if someone other than you could have hurt Hailey."

David continued to stare at the floor.

"All any of us want is the truth. Especially Officer McGee. I know him. He won't sleep at night until he finds out what really happened. He thought that might be important to you, too." She let that thought hang in the air for a moment.

"I'm not going to lie. If you killed Hailey we're going to find out and you're going to have to pay for it. But, David, no one wants to ruin your life if you're innocent."

The kid looked up now. "Ruin my life? Hailey's gone. I loved her. I was going to ask her to marry me this summer. Do you think I give a fuck what happens now?" He shook his head. "It just doesn't matter. My life *is* ruined."

Jordan swallowed, trying to figure out the best way to get through to him. He was in a state where he didn't give a rat's ass about anything. She'd been there, so she got it. "I know it feels like your life is over right now, but it might not always feel that way. It might take a few months, or it might take a few years to move on. If you didn't do this, if you didn't hurt her—"

"Look around." He stood and walked toward the cell bars. "They arrested me for killing Hailey. My *God*." Big tears streaked down his face. "Her parents hate me now. They're not even going to let me go to her funeral and say goodbye." He sobbed the words. "And all I can say is I don't remember what happened. That is *so* fucking lame. I want to say that I could never hurt her, even drunk, that I'd die before I laid a hand on her. But even if that's true, I'm just as guilty as the asshole who did this. I should have been there. I should have walked her home. I should have protected her."

He dropped his head against the bars and cried.

Jordan had never felt as she now did in any other interview. Most of the people she dealt with were deep inside the drug world, and most had rap sheets longer than her arm. Pity and sympathy weren't familiar sentiments in her line of work. Ty was right. Something about David Benson felt different.

She walked to the uniformed cop and asked him to open the cell door. David was still crying, so she touched his shoulder. "Hey, come on over here and sit down with me."

David scrubbed his hands up and down his face and followed her to the cot. He dropped down next to her. His long, lean body nearly doubled over as he sat with his elbows propped on his knees and his head hanging down. "I don't think I'm supposed to talk to you."

Jordan mirrored his pose and bumped her shoulder against his. "Probably not. Your dad will probably kick your ass. But only if he knows. I won't tell him if you don't."

David looked at her.

"And to make us even, Officer McGee is going to kick my ass, too. You see"—she pulled the recorder out of her pocket—"I'm supposed to ask for your permission to record our conversation and ask you to waive your rights to have your attorney present. I figure if you take a chance and talk to me, I'll take a chance, too."

Ty was going to snap her in half when she walked out with no recording, but she wasn't fishing for a confession. They needed one small thread to pull in a case that otherwise didn't add up. She smiled at him and slid Ty's recorder across the floor and out the front of the cell.

He looked puzzled, like he didn't quite know what to make of her. "You're not going to record our conversation? Are we going to get in trouble?"

"David, I hate to point out the obvious, but you're already in a shitload of trouble. And I spend most of my days with my ass in a sling for one reason or another, so I figure neither one of us has much to lose."

She smiled at him, trying to lighten his mood. "I've been told I'm resistant to authority. That's what they write in your review when you care more about getting the truth than you do about following the rules." She liked to believe her instincts were sharper than most and that guilt was not what she was feeling as she sat next to David Benson. "I believe there may be a truth here we haven't uncovered yet, and I'd like to talk to you about it. But the talking is up to you."

David took a deep breath and shrugged. "I don't care who I talk to anymore. I'm so tired, and I'm so confused. I don't even know what the truth is, so I don't see how this is going to help." His eyes filled with tears again. "I mean, I keep going over and over Friday night, thinking something else will pop into my head. Something that will make sense. Yet nothing ever does."

He sat back, his tall lanky body leaning against the cell wall. He looked exhausted. And he sounded heartbroken. Try as she might, Jordan was having a hell of a time believing he murdered his girlfriend and walked back to a frat house and slept it off.

"Here's my plan, David. Just for the next few minutes, let's operate under the assumption that you didn't kill Hailey."

He didn't look like the idea excited him much. "I may not have killed her, but I didn't protect her, either."

"David." She said his name sternly. She needed answers, and he needed to focus. "If you didn't kill her and you love her as much as you say you do, don't you think you owe it to her to find out what really happened?"

"I guess." He shrugged. "But it won't bring her back, and that's all I really want."

"Nothing is going to bring her back. That doesn't mean she doesn't deserve the truth. Her family deserves the truth. Hell, David, you deserve the truth."

Jordan shifted until her gaze made contact with his. "I'm going to tell you something that I never tell anyone. My parents were murdered when I was a kid. The circumstances were complicated, and what really happened has been kept from me for a very long time. I'm just now figuring out some of the details, but I can tell you the hardest thing to live without is the truth."

David nodded and said, "Okay."

"All right, let's back up a bit. Tell me what was going on in your lives a couple of weeks ago."

"A couple weeks ago?" he repeated. "I don't know. What do you mean? Everything was fine a couple weeks ago. Everything was fine until Friday night."

"Did Hailey recently mention that anyone was bothering her?"

He shook his head. "No."

"Think carefully, David. Did she mention another guy asking her out? Did she mention anyone that may have been jealous of you and her? Problems in her sorority house? Problems at home? Any of her belongings get mysteriously destroyed or go missing?"

"No, nothing. Everyone loved her." He was quiet for a minute. "I had some money and clothes stolen, but she never did, that I know of."

"How much money? And what kind of clothing?"

"Just the coat and hat. A few shirts. And about four hundred bucks."

Four hundred bucks was a good chunk of change for a college kid. "Did you report it?"

"No. It happened over the course of a few months. I live in a frat house, you know. If somebody spills beer, they just go to one of the rooms and pull out a shirt. We try to lock the bedroom doors, but most of the locks don't even work. There are always a million people in the house on weekends."

"What about the money? Did it go missing for everybody, or just you?"

"My roommate's money was gone once, too." He shrugged. "And I don't think he had anything to do with it. He's a good guy, even lent me some cash when mine was taken. Everybody knows who my dad is and that we're . . . well, you know. That money or clothes are not that hard for me to replace."

"What did your dad say?"

"To just use my debit card and stop keeping cash in my room. That's when my hat and coat went missing. It bugged me because my grandma gave me the coat for Christmas; I'd only had it a few weeks. Then some of my other clothes disappeared."

"Okay, let's focus on you then. Did you get into it with any of the other guys?"

David shook his head. "No. No fights at all."

"Maybe someone from another frat house? Any drunk jerk ever threaten you or Hailey? Anyone so jealous that they might hurt Hailey to get to you?"

A little more of the life seemed to drain out of him with her last question.

"Do you think someone could have killed her to hurt me or my dad? I mean, my dad's got business ties all over the state, probably all over the country."

"I think that's pretty unlikely, actually. I'm just trying to figure out if any recent situation felt off to you. Any person? Any event?"

"I can't think of anything." David was quiet for a moment. "Well, there was one weird thing that happened last week. Hailey said she saw me on campus Wednesday and that when she called my name and came toward me, I turned and walked away. She said she had to get to a class and didn't have time to chase me. She texted me and asked me what was wrong and why I was in the nursing building."

"Did you respond to her text?"

"I asked her what she'd been smoking because she knew I wouldn't be on campus that day. My dad broke ground on a new golf course community." He shrugged. "It's supposed to provide a lot of jobs, so the press was doing a story. Dad wanted me to be there."

"But Hailey thought she saw you?"

"Yeah. She was kind of wigged about it, because there aren't too many six four blond dudes walking around. I told her to get her eyes checked. We sort of joked about it until Friday night when . . ." David covered his eyes with his hands again. "God, I can't believe this is happening."

Ty watched Jordan step out of David Benson's cell and walk back down the hallway. "Well?"

She handed him his recorder. "Well, there's good news and bad news."

He raised a brow. "There's nothing on this recorder, is there?"

"That's the bad news. The good news is that I agree with you about David possibly being innocent. And I have a few things I think we should check out. But first you're going to buy me dinner."

Ten minutes later they were inside Antonio's Italian Restaurant ordering pizza.

"So he wouldn't let you record the conversation?" Ty asked.

"First thing he said was that I needed to contact his lawyer."

"You were with him for almost an hour."

Jordan nodded. "Let's face it, Ty. I wasn't there to interrogate a confession out of him. You didn't need me for that. I was there because your instincts are telling you more is going on here than a guy killing his girlfriend. After seeing him, I tended to agree. So I asked him if he just wanted to talk, off the record. He said okay. He seems like a good kid."

She leaned in with her elbows on the table. "I've dealt with a lot of assholes while working narcotics. I've also come across a few kids who got involved in something that spun out of control. Typically you can tell the difference." She waved one hand. "You know what I'm saying, right?"

Ty nodded. "Yeah, but this is a little different."

"It is, you're right," she agreed. "But from the moment I walked up to that cell, I didn't buy him as a killer. Some of my reaction is strictly experience, but there's more, too. Like when I met you, I knew you weren't capable of hurting me."

He narrowed his eyes. "What are you saying? I could be a badass if I wanted to."

Jordan threw her head back and chuckled that dark, sexy laugh that went all through him. "I'm sorry, cowboy, you are a badass. You're *my* badass. I just meant you weren't evil in that thug, drug-dealing sort of way." She leaned even closer and traced a finger across the back of his hand. "What I felt was much deeper, much more intense than anything I'd ever experienced with another man." She looked around and lowered her voice. "Probably why I had sex with you even though I barely knew your name."

He turned his hand over and held hers. "You keep telling yourself that, baby. I think you got caught in my McGee charm. But it's not your fault; no one can walk away from the McGee black magic."

"Quit being an asshole." She rolled her eyes and laughed. "I'm just saying there's a combination of things that shoot me to high alert when I'm dealing with someone dangerous. I'm not going to say that I know beyond a shadow of a doubt that David Benson isn't the world's best sociopath. Maybe he's just that good and he's duped us both, but I don't think so."

Ty was the one who leaned closer now. "So what do you make of the coat? You think he's telling the truth about it being stolen? Then there's your dream—you saw him do it."

"I know. But I'd think very hard about the possibility that someone is setting David Benson up." Jordan told him about the incident where Hailey claimed she saw David on campus.

Ty leaned back in the booth. "That's weird. I should check their phone records to see if he's telling the truth. If so, that would be quite a coincidence that for the second time in a week, witnesses are claiming that David Benson was in two different places at the same time."

"Maybe Lincoln University has cameras on campus. We could comb the footage to see if someone who looks like David was actually on campus while the real David was getting his picture taken with his dad in the next county."

The waiter approached and set their pizza on the table. Ty watched Jordan tease and joke with the young guy, but his mind was still going over her words. What motive could someone have for setting up David Benson?

When the waiter walked away, she asked, "You okay?"

"Yeah. I'm just trying to decide if I should try to stop David Benson's arraignment tomorrow morning. The kid is either a world-class liar or he's got a fucking clone walking around."

Jordan slid a piece of pizza onto his plate. "Eat. And go to the arraignment in the morning. I'm sure David's dad will have him bailed out and home on his cushy sofa before noon. Then you'll have time to pursue these other leads."

She wound a long, stringy glob of cheese around her finger and seductively licked it off. "Until then, I guess it will just be my job to take your mind off the case."

CHAPTER 14

Jordan rolled over and squinted at the clock when Ty's phone rang. It had just turned six. The water was running in the bathroom, so she carried Ty's phone to him.

"Sorry," he said around a mouthful of toothpaste. "I forgot to grab it off the nightstand."

"No kidding," she teased. "That damn thing goes off earlier than the alarm clock most mornings."

He wiped his mouth and looped his arms around her waist. "I'm sorry. I was going to let you sleep in. It's Friday and your last full day of vacation."

She returned his hug and then wrapped her arms around his neck. "Thank God. All this vacation time is about to kill me. I've managed to get roped into a mortgage." She looked down when Beauty pushed between their legs. "And adopt a very emotionally needy dog. Then I got mixed up in your murder case. I can't wait to get back to work where it's just normal run-of-the-mill drug dealers."

Ty's phone rang again.

Jordan brushed her teeth while he was talking. She knew from his end of the conversation that something big had happened.

"What's up?" She asked when he tossed the phone down.

"You are not going to believe this. An officer from Cooper was transporting David Benson to the court house and their car got run off the road. The officer is being airlifted to the hospital, but David is gone."

"Gone?"

"That's what Chief Donner said. He wants me to talk to David's dad, determine if he had anything to do with busting David out of custody. Isobel thought we were done when we arrested David. She's gone back home, close to an hour away. I could call her, but I'd rather not. The chief didn't have a problem with you questioning David yesterday. So you want to ride along again today?"

Jordan wasn't about to argue. If Ty never called Cherry-bomb again, all the better. "If Donner is okay with it, I wouldn't miss it."

An hour later, Ty pulled up to the gated entrance of the Benson estate.

"Holy crap." Jordan took off her sunglasses to get a better look. "This is more like a castle than a house. Doyle Benson probably has a million little rooms and tunnels he could hide David in."

"He's not here," Ty answered. "His old man is not that stupid."

"Agreed. And that's why I don't think it makes any sense for Doyle Benson to do this." Jordan said. "Why not just wait until after the arraignment and bail has been set? Then you walk away and there's no manhunt. It'd be a hell of a lot easier to flee the country then versus now."

Ty rolled down his window and hit a button labeled *service*.

"Yeah, but who knows what people do when they're desperate."

May I help you? echoed through the speaker.

"Officer McGee and associate here to speak with Doyle Benson." Ty flashed his badge for the small camera.

They drove through the gate, Jordan shaking her head at Ty the whole way.

"What?" he asked after he parked the truck.

"That's what you're calling me these days? Your associate?"

He grinned and tapped her nose. "Sounded more professional than my main squeeze." They got out of the truck and headed to the front door. "And less bizarre than my personal psychic."

"Fuck you," she said, but laughed as she said it.

The big wooden door was opened by an older woman dressed in a maid's uniform.

"I'm sorry, Mr. Benson is in a meeting. Can I take a message for him?"

"Yes, ma'am. Please tell him I'm sorry to interrupt, but we're going to need to speak with him here or I'll have to take him to the station for questioning."

Jordan rolled her eyes when the maid walked away. "Does everyone buy that polite bullshit you shovel at them?"

"Most of 'em." He winked. "Hey, you have your approach, I have mine."

Doyle Benson yanked the door open with attitude spilling out of every pore. "You can send anyone you'd like and haul me anywhere you'd like. I've already called my lawyer. He'll tell you exactly what I've already told Chief Donner. I have no idea where David is, but this joke of a legal system had better find him fast."

"Mr. Benson," Ty started, "we're trying to help."

"By arresting my son for a crime he didn't commit? Then involving him in a car accident and losing track of him? For all you know, he's lying dead in a ditch somewhere." Benson pushed the door closed.

Jordan stuck her boot inside, keeping the door ajar. Benson wrenched the door open again and lunged forward as if he wanted to reach out and strangle her.

"Back off, Benson." Ty pushed in front of Jordan. His voice was laced with a dangerous edge.

Her heart pounded at how swiftly he reacted. In equal measure, him treating her like an inept female instead of a cop frosted her ass.

"I have questions about David's disappearance," Ty said.

"Are you crazy?" Benson lashed out. "You think I'd involve my own son in a car accident? If I wanted to bust him out of jail, I certainly wouldn't have done it like that."

"We believe David may be innocent, Mr. Benson," Jordan said from behind Ty's big body.

Ty glared at her over his shoulder.

Benson also shifted to meet her gaze. She wouldn't have called his expression warm, but she'd peaked his interest. She ducked under Ty's big arm to slide in front of him again.

"I don't think you caused the car accident, either. Still, Officer McGee and I need to come inside and ask you some questions. Important questions that might help David."

"He arrested David." Benson stabbed a finger in Ty's direction. "And I don't even know who you are."

Jordan pulled out her badge. "I'm Detective Jordan Delany with the St. Louis PD. I'm consulting because I'm a narcotics detective and I've had extensive experience with young adults and crimes involving drugs and alcohol."

Benson didn't say anything. And although she was pretty sure Ty wanted to duct tape her mouth shut, he didn't say anything, either. She'd tipped their hand and said too much, but she knew that it was the only way to get Benson to cooperate.

"We've gone over and over this case, and I spoke with David last night," she admitted. She thrust her hand out when Benson started to object. "David is an adult, Mr. Benson. I advised him of his rights and told him he didn't have to speak with me. But he chose to let me help because he wants the truth."

"You people wouldn't know the truth if it ran over you."

"Really?" she said. "Because I think David had an alcohol-induced blackout the night Hailey was killed. And even so, after talking to David last night, I think someone may be trying to set him up. But I'm going to have a hell of a time proving that without your help."

Benson took a deep breath, then begrudgingly waved them in. They followed him into a big, luxurious room that had that look of perfection—dark wood, expensive looking furniture—more like a Hollywood set than a home.

Benson dropped down in one of the chairs and motioned for her to sit, but ignored Ty completely.

She figured Ty was fuming, especially since he was the one who'd always believed David was innocent. But he was also the one who arrested David, so Benson wasn't cutting him any slack. Which put her in the role of good cop. Not her preferred role, but she went with it. "Mr. Benson, for the record, do you know anything about David's escape from custody?"

Benson shook his head. "Of course not. And to my knowledge, it wasn't an escape. He was involved in a car accident."

She nodded. "Okay."

"I want to know where my boy is." Benson looked over at Ty. "If he is harmed in any way, I will own you and every other inept cop in this town."

"Look . . ." Ty began.

Jordan shook her head, hoping Ty understood the universal sign for shut the hell up. She could feel the tension spike every time Benson glared at Ty.

"Mr. Benson," she said to refocus David's father back on her, "you need to understand something. Officer McGee was not the only investigator working the case. An entire team gathered evidence and presented it to the DA. The DA's office decides whether an arrest is made or not. And on the surface, the case against David is solid."

Doyle Benson looked between her and Ty. "David was crazy about Hailey. I don't care how drunk he was, he wouldn't have hurt her. I know my son."

"Okay, then you need to answer a few questions and help us try to gather the evidence that would support his innocence."

Benson's gaze locked onto hers. His aggression eased back as he considered how to help his son. "Fine."

"If we operate on the assumption that David is innocent, the only thing that makes sense is that someone is trying to set him up. Is there anyone you can think of who has a grudge against David?"

Benson shook his head. "He's a good kid. He'd never hurt anyone."

"Maybe not intentionally, but what about jealousy? Did he earn a scholarship someone else needed? Did he date a girl someone else wanted?"

Benson sat quietly rubbing the bridge of his nose, his focus elsewhere. "I don't know. I can't think of anything like that."

Ty sat in one of the chairs and gestured at Benson. "Maybe this is about you. The best way to hurt a parent is through their child. Have you made any business enemies? Cost someone a lot of money? Fired someone and cost them their livelihood?"

"I know I've got people out there who hate what I do. There are always the nature lovers who complain if you cut down a tree to build homes or a golf course. But we try to be as friendly to the environment as possible. And I only hire and fire a handful of people, top management. I let human resources handle the rest. I don't know of anything that would be a reason to target David viciously enough to kill his girlfriend."

Jordan had to agree. Either David was guilty, or someone had a deeply personal grudge against him.

"Do you have relatives that may resent you?" Ty asked. "Have you turned someone down for a loan? Refused to help anyone's son or daughter go to college? Refused to pay for a wedding or a funeral?"

"Nothing like that." Benson took a deep breath and rubbed his forehead. "David and I don't have a lot of family. His grandparents are it, and they're crazy about him. After David's mother passed, her parents passed too. So there's no one on her side of the family that we still have contact with."

"When she passed, was there anyone who blamed you, or maybe challenged you for custody of David?" Ty asked.

"God, no. I'm David's father. Ann and I went through hell to have a child of our own. I would never let anyone take him from me. I may be a busy single dad, but David has always come before anything else in my life. Always."

Jordan glanced at Ty. She wasn't sure why, but Benson's words threw up a red flag. "What do mean that you went through hell to have David?"

"David is adopted. We tried for years to have a baby and it wasn't happening for us. Tests revealed that Ann had a tumor on her ovary. It was cancerous. She beat it the first time, but we knew we'd never have a child biologically, so we adopted."

"Was there anything unusual about David's adoption?"

"Not really. Not anything bad, anyway. We began with an agency that had us on a waiting list for years. I got frustrated, began to research again, and found a private adoption agency that said they could get us a baby in just months since we already had all our paperwork in order. But we got a call in a few weeks."

"A few weeks? I've never known an adoption to go through that quickly." Jordan could feel Ty's glare urging her on to the next question. "Forgive me for asking this, Mr. Benson, but did you offer someone at the adoption agency money to get you a child faster?"

"No, it wasn't like that. We paid the standard fees, no more than we were willing to pay with the other agency. Of course we offered to pay healthcare and food and housing for the birth mother while she was pregnant as an incentive, but that's a fairly standard practice."

"What agency did you go through?"

"Appleton in St. Louis. I worked with Mr. Appleton himself. When he called, he said there'd been a tragic accident. That a set of adoptive parents were in a fatal car accident. The agency wanted to assure the birth mother that her healthcare bills would be paid and her child would go to a loving home. He said he thought of us first because we had everything in order. It felt like fate. Not that we were happy anyone died, but we'd been waiting a long time for a child."

Benson's gaze darted between Jordan and Ty. "I'm telling you, no one challenged anything. I swear it was perfectly legal and in the best interest of everyone. You don't honestly think David's adoption has something to do with all this, do you? That was over twenty years ago."

"Probably not," Ty said. "But we should check it out anyway. We're going to need all the information you have regarding David's adoption."

"Something about this adoption thing stinks." Ty pulled out of the Bensons' security gate, fingers tapping on the steering wheel. "People wait for years to adopt a child. Was it dumb luck that the Bensons got a child in a few weeks after signing with Appleton, or were they so fed up with waiting that they offered someone a huge sum of money for a child?"

"You think Benson is lying?" Jordan asked.

"Not sure. And even if he is, I'm not sure why it would matter. Or why would it impact his son's life twenty years later."

Jordan shrugged. "Maybe someone knew about it and has been holding a grudge. Yet I can't imagine why they'd wait twenty years and then take it out on David. Wait . . . *oh shit*."

Ty glanced at her. "What?"

"I just had a thought. What if this *is* about money? Try this on for size: Let's say the adoptive parents *didn't* die in a fatal accident. What is the other scenario that would make an extra baby suddenly available?"

"So now we're playing twenty questions?"

She smacked his arm. "Think about it; it's the only thing that makes sense."

"What?"

"Two babies."

"Twins?" he said. "Jesus, Jordan, you watch too many late night movies."

"Maybe, but think about it." She turned off the radio and shifted in her seat. "Let's say you have a birth mom, and whoops, she has twins when you were only expecting one baby. It was twenty years ago, and maybe technology wasn't as good or she was dirt poor and didn't have good healthcare. Who knows why, but shit happens. Whatever the reason, they expected only one baby and instead got two. So how do you make your agency an extra fifty grand? That's about what it costs to adopt a kid, right?"

Jordan was on a roll. Ty loved watching her come alive.

"I guess," he agreed. "Could be even more if you offer to pay all the expenses."

"Exactly. So you tell the birth mom that the adoptive parents are surprised but thrilled to have twins. She goes on her happy way thinking her kids are in a loving home. But you really only give one of the babies to the new parents, because, hey, you've got this other wealthy family just chomping at the bit for a kid. You know the rich bastard will hand over the cash fast, so you go to him and play a song and dance about a tragic accident—*for a cool fifty grand, I can get you a kid in a few weeks.* Who's the wiser? Birth mom is happy. Adoptive parents A are happy because they got the kid promised to them, and you've made wealthy adoptive parents B super happy. Plus you scored a bunch of extra cash for yourself."

"That's a pretty far out theory. But it would explain a lot."

"Man"—Jordan poked him—"why don't I ever think of clever shit to score big bucks and still make everyone happy?"

"Uh, maybe because you don't want to spend years and years in jail."

"Maybe," she muttered. "But he likely thought he was doing everyone a favor. Including himself."

"Let's say that all this is true. That means you also believe that David has an evil twin who's after him. Why? How would he even know he had a twin? And how does any of this make sense?"

Jordan stewed in her seat for a minute. "Well, maybe . . . Hey, I can't do all your work for you. Some shit you have to figure out on your own. But maybe there are two David Bensons walking around out there. Maybe Hailey *did* see someone on campus who looked like David. Maybe your witness did see another David lurking outside the sorority house at the same time the real David was heaving his guts up outside the frat house."

"Okay, Nancy Drew, get your phone out. You know what's next, right?"

"Yeah, yeah. I'm already looking up the address for the Appleton Adoption Agency."

CHAPTER 15

Jordan didn't plan on telling Ty—it was too much fun giving him shit about living in the boonies—but she was really starting to enjoy the long drive between Longdale and St. Louis. All her life she'd lived in the city or suburbs, but driving through the rural communities and open spaces of Missouri held a certain peacefulness she hadn't experienced before. Ty, on the other hand, seemed to grow more and more restless as they drove into the city.

"What's wrong?" she finally asked.

"This part of St. Louis makes me twitchy."

He pulled his oversized black F-350 into a parking garage in Clayton, Missouri. The upper-class business district was home to many a law agency, government office, and, more importantly, the Appleton Adoption Agency.

Jordan scanned the surroundings looking for something suspicious. "Why? This is a beautiful, upscale town. No one will bother your precious truck while we're inside," she teased. "I promise."

"It's not that. Just look around. There are too many buildings on top of one another. Too many corporate guys in three-piece suits. All these sleek, expensive cars. I feel like Shrek, the big bumbling ogre who's stumbled into the wrong part of the village."

She laughed. "You are *so* weird."

But she took in his appearance from head to toe, recognizing that he was right—no one was ever going to mistake him for a corporate geek. His dark hair and sultry gray eyes looked perfectly at home in a standard button-down shirt and jeans. His black leather jacket and boots matched his big, black truck.

"I think you look badass and sexy." And thankfully nothing like the three suits that just walked by. She leaned over and kissed him. Then she slid out of his truck and took his hand as they walked to the adoption agency. "Don't worry, honey, I'm armed. Just in case anyone comes after you with a pitchfork."

They entered the plush Appleton offices, and Ty approached the receptionist. "Hi. I'm Officer Tyler McGee." He flashed one of those killer bad-boy smiles along with his badge. "We need to speak with Blake Appleton. Are we in the right spot?"

The receptionist actually did a double take when she saw Ty smiling down at her. "You sure are." She smiled back. "But I'm afraid he's in a meeting right now. Can I ask what this is regarding?"

Jordan flashed her badge, too. "A homicide. Ask him if he'd like to take a few minutes now, here, or make arrangements to come to the police department later."

Ty turned to her when the lady walked away. "I was trying to be nice. You're messing with my mojo."

"You were flirting, pretty boy. We don't have time for you to make nice with the receptionist."

He shook his head. "We might have to get you some therapy for your jealousy issues."

She narrowed her eyes and flipped him off. "I don't need therapy. I have a gun."

The receptionist returned and led them into a conference room. "Mr. Appleton will be here shortly."

Blake Appleton entered a few minutes later. He was a short older man. Maybe in his fifties.

Ty held out his hand. "Mr. Appleton, I'm Officer Tyler McGee. This is Detective Jordan Delany. We're investigating a murder that may be related to one of your adoptions. Do you have any memory of the Ann and Doyle Benson adoption?"

By the cool look Appleton focused on Ty, Jordan suspected he remembered it well. "I remember Mr. Benson and his wife, yes. But it was a closed adoption. The records are sealed and can't be opened without a court order, not even for the police."

Jordan watched the shift in Ty's body language, an almost imperceptible slide from easygoing to quiet predator. "Well, let me ask some questions in general; we won't say it's about any particular case."

Appleton remained quiet.

"If parents who were looking to adopt were wealthy, had more financial resources to contribute to a birth mother than other prospective parents, would there be less waiting time for a child?"

"I'm sure you know, as an officer of the law, it is illegal to buy a child in any way, shape, or form. That said, some adoptive parents are able to financially support birth mothers more fully than others."

"Have you ever had an incident where it turned out that there were twins instead of just one baby? What would you do in that situation, Mr. Appleton?" Jordan asked.

Appleton stiffened. "What are you getting at, Detective?"

"We have suspicions that the boy adopted by the Bensons has a twin." Ty was direct. He leaned forward and went for the kill. "We also suspect if something like that happened, you'd remember it well since your adoption agency could collect two fees off of the same birth mom without her ever knowing."

"I pair birth mothers who are unable to care for their child with parents who long for a child. I have never done anything unethical or illegal, and, as I said, our records are sealed."

"Okay, since you can't divulge that one important piece of information without a court order, I'll get that court order." Ty leaned back in the chair and folded his arms. "I'll be more than happy to tell the judge I'm investigating a murder and that I believe your agency is smack dab in the middle of it. I will suggest that David Benson has a twin and that you knew it. Not only knew it, but profited because of it. And while I'm at it, I'll make damn sure investigators get in here and comb through your adoptions so extensively that if adoptive parents so much as bought you a stick of gum under the table, we'll know about it. You better pray to God you kept good records."

Appleton looked like he wanted to puke, and Jordan couldn't say she blamed him. Ty radiated a lethal intimidation. The twin theory had been an educated guess on her part, but Ty had gone all in, gambling that Appleton knew something.

"I didn't do what you're accusing me of," Appleton finally said.

"Then I guess you've got nothing to worry about." Ty turned to Jordan. "Are you ready, Detective?"

"And if I tell you what I remember, then what?" Appleton asked.

"Then I go away and I have no reason to meet with a judge. I'm investigating a homicide. I don't give a damn how you make money. Unless you stand in my way," Ty added.

Several moments passed before Appleton spoke again. "I think David Benson might have a twin," Appleton conceded.

Ty shifted his gaze to Jordan. She watched him swallow down the disbelief. Honestly, she was having a hard time choking it down herself. Of all the crazy crap she'd been wrong about lately, this was a hell of a thing to be right about.

"But you're wrong about how the whole thing played out. I didn't sell another baby to make a profit or gain additional fees. I'd never do that. The birth mom came to me like they all come to me—too young, too scared, or too poor to raise a child. It's never a simple decision for a birth mother."

Appleton went to a cabinet and retrieved three bottles of water and placed them on the table. "This particular mother was poor, well below poverty level. She said she couldn't raise the baby. She was almost seven months along when she came to me. I talked to her for a long time, and she finally admitted she was about to be evicted from her apartment. She asked if I could get her immediate living expenses."

"And you knew the Bensons would be all over that for a chance to have a baby."

Appleton nodded. "Yes. I started the wheels in motion, and I backdated some of the documents and counseling sessions so the adoption would go through. The Bensons were a good family. Their paperwork was perfect, and they'd already jumped through every hoop an adoptive family needs to jump through. I knew if I told them another set of parents had died in a car accident, they had the financial resources to cover any medical bills, and yes, I knew they'd even offer to cover the previous seven months of the mother's living expenses."

"Go on," Ty said when Appleton grew quiet.

Appleton took a long swig from his bottle of water. "Not long after that she delivered at home. She said her sister had been there to help, but there was a snowstorm and she claimed she couldn't get to the hospital. So I sent an ambulance to pick her and the baby up. I got them checked out at the hospital and everything went smoothly from that point on. The Bensons got their child, the birth mother got her bills covered and a good chunk of change for living expenses.

"I decided to hand deliver her final check. I felt like I had pushed things through quickly, so I thought I'd offer her more of our ongoing counseling sessions as well as see how she was doing."

Appleton looked at Ty. "She came to the door with a baby in her arms. She looked guilty as hell, and I knew. Well, I suspected she'd been pregnant with twins and given up one to support herself and the other child. I think that's why she delivered at home."

"But you didn't tell anyone?" Ty asked.

"She claimed she was babysitting for a friend, so I let it go." Appleton shook his head. "I wrestled with my suspicions for a long time. She'd made thousands off the Bensons in living expenses by the time it was over and she got to keep one of her babies, too. So she was happy. The Bensons were thrilled to finally be parents. The only one who had a problem with it was me. So I just kept quiet."

"Do you remember her name?" Ty asked.

Appleton nodded. "Misty Williams."

There was more than one Misty Williams in Missouri. Even with police databases, it had been difficult to narrow their search to the right woman. But by the process of elimination, Ty was pretty sure he was on the right trail. Her last known address was a P.O box in Daisyville. Population thirty-one.

The woman had obviously lived off the radar. As far as Ty could tell, she was damn good at it.

He and Jordan had been driving back roads for more than an hour when they came upon a gas station just inside the Daisyville town limits. He pulled in and smiled when he read the sign: Local Yokel Pit Stop.

"Look, baby. We can get gas, donuts, fishing bait, and ammunition all at the same place. Hot damn."

"I have to pee, and I am *so* not doing it in there."

"Then you ain't doing it for quite a while. This is the only public building we've passed in miles."

Jordan glared at him. "Seriously? How did I get here, and what have you done with my real life? I am never, and I mean never ever, getting involved with one of your backwoods cases again."

"Come on, now. The twin thing was your revelation, not mine." He laid a hand on her thigh. "If you're a good girl and go pee-pee, I'll buy you a chocolate Long John and some bullets."

She swatted his hand away. "You're a disturbed individual. Let's just get the info we need and get the hell out of here."

Jordan followed him inside and scowled when he pointed to the restroom sign. But she hiked up her jeans and stomped to the far corner of the building.

He grabbed a couple of bottled waters and waited for Jordan so they could pump the cashier for information.

"Was it as bad as you thought?" he asked when she came out.

"Worse," she grumbled.

They walked to the register.

"Hi, there," the cashier said. "Will this do it for you?"

"Yes, ma'am" Ty answered. "Except I was wondering if you could point me in the right direction. I had a distant cousin that I lost touch with when we were kids. Her name was Misty Williams. I tried to look her up, and all I could find was a P.O. box in Daisyville. Am I in the right spot?"

"Sure are," the woman said. "But no one has seen hide nor hair of Misty in probably two years. For a while we kind of wondered if maybe she had passed, but her son still comes in every few weeks and picks up food and mail. I asked him if his momma was okay. He said she had a bad leg and it was hard for her to get around."

Jordan gave Ty a playful punch in the arm. "You didn't tell me Misty had a son. What's his name?"

"I'm not sure." Ty scratched his chin. "Like I said, I haven't seen Misty in years. I think she may have been pregnant the last time I saw her. That was probably what? Twenty years ago?"

"The boy's name is Jeb," the woman answered. "And you're right, he's probably nineteen or twenty, I guess. Nice kid. Real quiet, though." She leaned forward like she was letting them in on a huge secret. "I think because Misty home-schooled him, he's real backwards. They both are nice enough, just not too social."

"Well, thanks for the chat." Ty winked and smiled at the woman behind the counter. "That's too bad you haven't seen Misty around lately. Maybe I should try to find Jeb and make sure they don't need anything. You don't happen to know where they live, do you?"

"I've never been there, but I hear their trailer is about five miles up Salty Spring Road. It's a horrible tiny twister of a dirt road. If that's your truck out there, I wouldn't recommend you try it at night."

※

"We are in serious *Deliverance* territory. All we're missing is a banjo and Burt Reynolds," Jordan murmured as Ty snaked his big-ass truck along the narrow dirt road.

"Fuckin' A, we are. Good thing it's dark." Ty tapped the brakes as something with fur and four legs dashed out in front of them. "It'd be really scary if we could actually see what's around us."

Ty liked guns almost as much as he liked his truck, so Jordan was pretty sure he'd be well armed. "What are you carrying?"

"My Sig. And I have a rifle and a Colt behind the seat. You?"

"Just my Glock. I didn't bring a backup. Now I kind of wish I had. I thought us city slickers had problems with all of our drugs and gangs and robberies, but we've got nothing on you country folk. I've got an ugly premonition about being naked and chained to some psychopath's water heater with a ball gag in my mouth."

Ty chuckled. "If that's a fantasy of yours, I'm sure we can work something out."

"No one has seen Misty in two years. You know why? Because Jeb probably had a psychotic break from being forced to live in the ass-end of nowhere his whole life. Sounds like she didn't even let him go to school. He probably got fed up and put her in the wood chipper."

Ty shook his head. "A lot of people enjoy living in remote areas, baby. It's peaceful."

She was working on another smart remark when Ty's headlights reflected off something shiny. "Stop. Look over there, just to the right. The woman at the gas station said about five miles up."

"We're at four point eight. Let's pull off and check it out." Ty pulled the truck over and killed the lights. Then he turned and reached for a backpack on the back seat. "Grab your gun and take this." He handed her a flashlight. "The moon is fairly bright, so let's try not to turn these on until we figure out if this is his place and if he's here or not. Come on."

She slid out of the truck, straight into mud. This probably wasn't the time to throw out that he owed her one big whopping Caribbean vacation. But if they survived the excursion to Freddy Krueger's trailer, she sure as hell intended to remind him.

Locked and loaded, they crept closer, dodging and stepping over weeds, wood, and wreckage that may have been, at one time, car parts. Everything else that was crunching beneath their feet, she didn't care to inspect too closely.

They took cover behind a large tree next to a dilapidated and rusted old trailer.

"Stay down right here and cover the door," Ty whispered. "I'm going around to the back to see if I can get a look inside. Listen for noise and watch for lights, but I don't think anyone's here."

"You can't be sure no one is here just because there are no lights or noise," she whispered back.

"I'm sure because no one has shot at us yet."

"Swell," she mumbled. But she'd been thinking the same thing.

Ty returned a couple minutes later. "Anything?" she asked.

"I don't think he's here, but there's a smell coming from inside that can't be right. I'm going in to check it out. We might as well be sure this place is empty since we've come this far."

"Yeah, cause you sure as shit aren't getting me back out here again."

"Once I've cleared it, I'll come get you." He grabbed her arm and slipped the truck keys into her jacket pocket. "If shots are fired, take off and drive until you have enough reception to call Jonesy."

"Fuck off. If you wanted arm candy instead of backup, you should have brought Stinkerbelle. Right now I'm a cop, not your girlfriend. We go on three. You clear right, and I'll go left."

He wanted to argue, she knew by the barely audible *stubborn-ass woman* he muttered. But a second later he nodded.

They eased up to the front door of the trailer, and Ty positioned himself to kick it in. When it flew open, the stink flew out. In spite of the foul odor, they entered and swept through the place.

Clearing the small, jam-packed trailer wasn't as easy as one would imagine. There was as much crap littering the inside as there was outside. And it was darker than pitch. Luckily, the place was only the size of a Cracker Jack box, so it didn't take long to search all possible hidey-holes. But the smell continued to be a deadly beast wafting through the air.

After Jordan checked out a small room on the left and what may have been at one time a kitchen, she called out, "Clear."

"Clear," Ty echoed. "Jesus al-mighty *damn*, what reeks?"

Rotten food. Feces. One nauseating smell tried to overpower the other. But on top of it all, a foul layer of stale smoke permeated everything. And *that* was the smell Hailey had been trying to make Jordan understand. She was certain of it.

"Ah shit," she heard Ty grumble.

Fearing that someone may have surprised him, she raised her gun and moved quietly to the tiny bedroom he'd entered. Her heart hammered as she aimed the flashlight and gun together and swept in. But Ty was alone, shining his light around the room.

"You scared the crap out of me," she said. "I thought someone or some*thing* got you. Like maybe a giant man-eating rat."

"We got bigger problems than rats. Take a look around. He's got a whole room wallpapered with pictures of David Benson."

CHAPTER 16

"Well, looky here," Jordan moved her flashlight from one horrifying collage of pictures to the next. "We've got ourselves a real hard-core nutcase, wouldn't you say, Officer McGee?"

"Damn." Ty whistled long and low. "This is like entering a bad slasher movie about three seconds before one of us gets our heads lobbed off. Maybe we should back out, make some phone calls, and get a team up here before psycho-boy comes back."

Jordan continued to shine her flashlight around the room, concentrating mostly on the newspaper clippings. "He's not coming back. He hasn't been back, in my estimation, in about a month."

Ty turned the flashlight on his face as though he were getting ready to tell a scary story around the campfire. "This dude makes the whack job in *Silence of the Lambs* look like a pillar of society. How could you possibly guess what his next move is or when he was last here?"

She followed suit and shined her light up at her face. "My spidey senses are amazing."

Unamused, Ty continued to stare.

"Okay, fine." She shined the flashlight at a few of the newspaper clippings. "Look at the dates. That says January 7th. That one's from December. That one looks like the most recent, January 22nd."

Doyle Benson was big news in a little town. It looked like every time the man broke ground on another real estate deal or gave to charity, he ended up in the newspaper. David was often in the pictures, too.

"Look at all of these pictures and newspaper clippings, some going back a year or more. There are none about David being arrested for Hailey's murder. And it's been all over the news. Trust me, this kind of obsession doesn't just go away. Wherever he's holed up now, he's got just as many pictures and newspaper clippings about David there. He wouldn't be able to help himself."

"I don't disagree, but finding him is going to be difficult; he knows how to live under the radar."

Ty shined his light on picture after picture. David alone. David and his father. David and Hailey. "He's apparently obsessed with David."

Jordan stepped closer and looked at the bizarre number of pictures of David's clothing, David's car, David's hair. One whole wall was just David's mouth and smile. Close-ups of his teeth, to be exact. "No, he was studying David. Everything about him. What he wore. How his clothes looked. His Hair. But most importantly, his teeth. It was the one thing he couldn't copy."

Jordan shined the light on her face and turned to Ty. "Holy fucking bingo. That's what Hailey's been trying to show me. That the person who killed her wasn't David. Only I didn't get it. Chances are I never would have because details that specific are hard for me to understand from a dream. And on top of it, I didn't know what David's teeth looked like. Why would I?"

She turned back to the pictures. "But I've run my tongue over every one of yours. I know your smile better than I know my own. You can bet if your clone showed up with jacked-up teeth, I'd damn well know the difference. And Hailey knew the difference too."

Ty inched closer and studied the pictures of David's smile, too. "I guess when your old man is loaded, braces and a million-dollar smile aren't hard to come by."

Jordan nodded and shined her light on a smile that was obviously not David's, but Jeb's. "But when you live wondering if you're going to get to eat on any given day, braces are never going to be an option."

"Until you want to impersonate your rich brother," Ty added. "Shit. I thought he just wanted to screw with David and ruin his life. But do you think he actually wants to become David?"

"I'm not sure. I'm having trouble following Jeb's logic on this one."

He gestured at the images. "This place is going to need to be gone through with a fine-toothed comb, but I'm not touching any of it without a hazmat suit. From the stench, I'm guessing he kept using the john well after it had the ability to flush."

Jordan followed Ty back outside, both of them heaving fresh air into their lungs after they'd stepped several yards away from the trailer. "I hope we didn't just catch something in there," she said. She bent over with her hands propped on her knees, attempting to breathe through a wave of nausea.

"Yeah. Like the plague. I guess if I ended up living like that and my twin got the golden goose, I'd be a little pissed too. But that"—he pointed to the trailer—"is a young man too bat-shit crazy to save."

Satisfied that she wasn't going to be sick, Jordan stood upright. "Or he's just full of rage. You may be underestimating how resentful this guy is." Jordan thought for a second, remembered what it felt like to believe you'd gotten the raw end of a deal where a sibling was concerned. "What I'm going to say makes me sound like a god-awful bitch, but . . ." She took a deep breath and met Ty's gaze. "But a part of me always resented Katy. Especially right after the murders."

She never believed she'd admit such an ugly truth to anyone, but Ty had become her safe zone. It had happened when she wasn't looking, but every day she was less and less afraid he'd run from all her ugly truths. "To me, it seemed that Katy got a better deal. And all she really got was a gunshot to the head."

Ty stepped toward her. "Babe—"

"No, I'm fine. Really, I am. This isn't about me, but I want you to understand that it's easy to look at a sibling with jealousy and anger, even when there's nothing rational or logical about it. Katy was murdered. She was young and innocent and had nothing to do with what happened, but God forgive me, because none of that stopped me from hating her just a little bit. She got to be with my mom and dad, and once again, I felt tossed aside like the freak I was. I wasn't even worthy of being with them in death."

"Jordan, no one tossed you aside. Your mom was trying to save you."

"You're right. Absolutely. And now as a rational adult—and I will use that term loosely—I can see that. But for a long time I was really messed up about it. So I wonder how messed up a guy would be if he learned that his twin brother went to wealthy parents. That he lived in an amazing home, had amazing friends, horses, in-ground pool, drove amazing cars, and attended college without ever thinking about where the money would come from. *And* had braces to make his smile nothing less than radiant. Hell, Ty, I could hate David just a little bit, myself, for those reasons."

Ty sighed. "None of those things excuse what Jeb's doing. I don't care what his life was like; a shitty childhood is not an excuse to kill. And you know as well as I do, if he's the one that caused that accident this morning, David may already be dead." Ty raked his finger through his hair. "Let's head back to the truck."

When she followed him without another word, he stopped and turned to her. "What? You obviously have something to say and aren't saying it. You think what he's doing is okay because his childhood was crappy."

"I did *not* say that. I'm just saying I understand the reasoning behind the resentment."

"Well, I don't."

Ty's arrogant dismissal of relevant facts burned a hot streak through her ability to censor herself. "You don't understand because you lived like a member of the Brady Bunch all your life. Pies from grandma, horses on a beautiful farm, probably Disney vacations. Did you ever go without food? Did you ever sleep with one eye open because you were afraid someone was going to come into your bedroom and do bad things to you?"

Ty's breath burst out in a rush. "Christ," he murmured.

The night was dark, and his face was shadowed, but she knew she'd shocked him. And she wished like hell it was one ugly truth she'd kept to herself.

"Did someone hurt you?"

"No, not like you're thinking. But it wasn't for lack of trying. I was simply too damn mean for anyone to take advantage of. The point I'm trying to make is that I spent eight years in foster care. Most of them were okay. But I also know what it's like to be in a home where no one cares if you eat, or take drugs, or get assaulted by older foster kids. It's hard to care much about right or wrong when its survival of the fittest. What if Jeb Williams had an abusive, controlling nutcase for a mother and not much else? Maybe he's lived out here like a social deviant for so long that he's completely out of touch with reality.

Ty took her hand and led her to the truck. He opened the door, but before she could climb in, he pulled her against him. His arms slid around her waist and he held on. "I'm sorry," he whispered. "For all the horrible things you've been through."

"I'm not." She touched his cheek. "I think it might be karma. When life craps you down a long, hellish tunnel, the light at the end can be pretty spectacular." She laced her hands behind his neck, pulled his ear to her lips, and whispered, "Especially when that light has big muscles, big beautiful eyes, and a really big . . ." She reached down and stroked her fingers over his crotch, but then said, "Heart."

He kissed her cheek. "You're a beautiful disaster, you know that?"

She laughed as she hopped up into the truck. "But I'm your beautiful disaster. Aren't you lucky?"

When Ty slid into the driver's seat, she said, "You know, I like that. Nothing has ever summed up my life quite so accurately. I just might get that tattooed on my ass."

Ty looked at her and shook his head. "Wouldn't surprise me any." He started the truck and pulled back onto the dirt road. "But before we locate a tattoo parlor, we've got to drive until we get phone reception so I can get a crime scene unit out here. And um . . ."

"I know, I know. You've got to call Cherry-bomb because it was her case, too. I get it." Earlier hadn't felt like the right time to bring up vacation, but now certainly did. "But it's going to cost you. You owe me at least a week of beautiful, clear Caribbean water. And there'd better be no economy hotel. I'm talking five stars, spa, massage, room service."

"Okay. Geez, I get it. Don't get your panties in a twist again."

Jordan folded her arms and sat quietly. Her panties weren't necessarily twisted, but they were definitely bunched in all the wrong places. She forced her mind to something a bit more productive. "You know, with Hailey gone, and maybe David now, too, all Jeb would need to do is impersonate David for a few short months until the trial. He knows Doyle is going to spare no expense to get David off. Once he's acquitted, all he'd need to do is make sure Doyle dies in a nasty accident. Then Jeb could collect all of Doyle's money as David Benson, heir to the Benson real estate fortune. Who would ever question his identity?"

Ty took a deep breath and let it out slowly. "That's a seriously twisted plan."

"I think what we just witnessed qualifies as seriously twisted."

"True. He'd need to lay low and keep his distance from Doyle, make a conscious effort not to give himself away because of his teeth. Maybe he could pull it off, but I doubt it. It would be a hell of a gamble. Although I guess the worst case is he ends up in jail. And after seeing that trailer, jail would be a step up."

"And best case is that he ends up millions richer."

"Wow." Ty shook his head. "The kid may never have gone to school, but he wasn't stupid, was he?"

Jordan and Ty were sitting in front of Jeb Saunders's trailer on the tailgate of the truck when the first police units arrived. *Oh, lovely*, Jordan thought. She watched Isobel Riley slide out of her sleek, expensive SUV.

Jordan's nerve endings reacted like someone had not only clawed, but carved the top layer clean off a chalkboard.

Ty squeezed Jordan's hand and gave her a sideways glance as he slid to a stand. "Play nice, or I'll tattoo *mean girl* instead of *beautiful disaster* on your ass."

"I could take her in a heartbeat, you know," Jordan mumbled as she watched red-headed Isobel saunter closer in her stylish coat. "Snap her in half and leave her here for the crows."

"Let's not do that just yet." Ty gave her a quick peck on the cheek. "I'm planning to stick her here with the crime scene unit while you and I look for Jeb."

"Really?" Jordan's mood brightened. Until she noticed Isobel wasn't so much sauntering as blazing a trail toward Ty.

"What the hell, McGee? If you were going to investigate further, you had no right doing it alone."

"He wasn't alone," Jordan said mildly. "He had me."

Isobel turned a sharp glare on Jordan. "You are not an investigating officer on this case."

Jordan hopped off the tailgate and stepped toward Isobel. "Actually—"

Ty shot her a please-let-me-handle-this look. "Actually," he interrupted, "because Jordan is a St. Louis detective who specializes in controlled substances, Chief Donner agreed to let her act as a consultant since David claims to have blacked out from alcohol."

Isobel scowled at both of them. "Donner is an idiot and we both know it. I don't care what he says—*she* is not a part of this investigation."

Isobel stabbed a finger in Jordan's direction. "You can't make her a consultant just because you're screwing her."

"Watch it, Isobel." Ty's voice was low. It would have appeared deceptively calm to the average observer, but Jordan recognized the danger woven through the cool words.

"It's a conflict of interest to work with someone you're sleeping with." Isobel spat the words as if they left a foul taste in her mouth. "Fix it, or I'll report you."

"Then I'll have no choice but to report you." Jordan took one small step toward the redhead. "If screwing Ty is grounds for dismissal from this case, then you shouldn't be here either, should you?"

Isobel glanced up at Ty, no doubt stunned that he'd confessed the truth. And shocked further that she'd been called out on it. Then she turned a hateful glare on Jordan. "I am not screwing him."

"Only because he said no this time. But you gave it the good old college try, didn't you? If you want to go down the conflict of interest road, you'll be answering just as many questions as we will."

Isobel turned and stomped off.

Jordan looked up at Ty. "It appears I pissed in her Wheaties."

He was fighting a smile. "I told you to be nice."

"No, you said don't be mean. There's a difference. If I were mean, I'd have pointed out that you actually called *me* after you banged me. But I took the higher road."

Ty took her hand. "I'm sorry she talked to you that way; she had no right. I'd have never gotten this far without you."

"You would have. It might have taken a little longer, but you were the one that believed David was innocent all along. I'm supposed to be psychic, and I still got it wrong."

"I'm going to ask her what the hell her problem is."

Jordan held on to his hand when he tried to walk away. "No, it's fine. What's the point? It'll just make things harder for you. And we both know what her problem is." She winked. "It's impossible to walk away from that McGee black magic." Jordan reached into his pocket and pulled out his keys. "In fact, just let it go. Tell her you got rid of me. I'll head back to town and locate Doyle Benson. He needs to know the truth and that he and David are in danger."

Ty put his arms around her in a quick hug and kissed her temple. "I'll have everyone briefed and set to go here inside a half hour. Then I'll be right behind you." He stepped back and pinned her with a warning glare. "Do nothing but talk to Benson, you got it? I don't care what lead you think you come across. No heroics without backup. Take no action without talking to me first."

She smiled. He was just so damn sexy when he tried to give her orders.

"I mean it, Jordan. You do nothing dangerous without me, are we clear?"

"It's almost like you're channeling Bahan." She backed up a few steps. "It's kind of cool. And yet somehow very disturbing." She winked again and crossed her heart. "I'll be careful."

It wasn't a hollow promise. Jordan had nothing more in mind than talking with Doyle Benson. She'd attempted to call him with no success, so she continued to drive to his estate.

But as she approached his home, she watched a sleek Audi R8 speed through the Benson security gates and take off down Highway Z. Doyle Benson was blazing a trail to somewhere in a big hurry.

She stayed well behind him; Ty's truck wasn't exactly a subtle trailing vehicle. But if Doyle caught sight of her, he never showed it. She clocked him at well over ninety. What the hell was going on? Could Jeb be luring Doyle Benson into a disastrous fate already?

She dialed Ty. His voicemail came on.

"Hey, don't be pissed, but I'm tailing Doyle Benson going damn near a hundred miles an hour west on Highway Z. I've got a sneaking suspicion Jeb may be behind it. I'll text you when we stop."

Doyle slowed and turned into a new condo community under construction. If Jeb was here, the last think she wanted to do was spook him. So she eased off the gas, drove past the entrance by a couple hundred feet, and parked on the shoulder of the highway. Ty was going to have her hide for parking Molly in such a high-traffic area. If his precious truck ended up with so much as a chip on the windshield, she'd never hear the end of it.

She climbed through a tree-lined spot and watched Doyle Benson enter one of the units under construction. She texted Ty.

I think Jeb has lured Doyle Benson into a trap. I'm following Benson inside a condo unit in his Cedar Springs Development off Highway Z. There's a Bobcat in front of the condo he entered.

It was just before five a.m. on a Saturday morning. The place was a ghost town.

She pulled her gun and opted to step quietly through a window opening in lieu of using the front door. Voices from the next floor caught her attention. She eyed the unfinished stairs and hoped like hell they didn't creak under her weight.

She crept up the staircase one stair at a time. The voices were louder now. She eased to a stop outside one of the rooms.

"What the hell is going on here?" Doyle Benson demanded. Then he screamed David's name and a gunshot rang out.

Jordan had no choice but to enter. "Police. Freeze. Put your arms in the air."

There were two David Bensons all right. It was damn weird seeing them side by side, but she had no problem telling them apart. David dropped to the ground holding his father while Jeb pointed his gun at her.

"Slowly put the gun on the ground. Arms in the air," she ordered.

"You put it down," the kid shouted back. Then the little fucker squeezed off a round that narrowly missed her head. She dove behind a stack of plywood as he shot off two more rounds.

"Oh God, Dad. Please help him. Please, Dad, please. Oh God, don't die."

Jordan heard the pleas and knew they were David's tearful cries.

"Jeb, put down the gun," she called out. "It's over. Your plan isn't going to work."

"Sure it is," he screamed. "I'm going to be David Benson, the hero. Everyone knows what a greedy bastard Doyle Benson is. When I tell the cops I figured out my dad killed Hailey to keep me from marrying her, they'll never convict me for shooting him in self defense."

So the kid did have a plan. Not a great one, but Jeb actually *was* planning to kill David and Doyle and end up with their money.

She heard another keening cry from David.

"Jeb, every officer in the county is on the way here right now. I'm a cop. I've been to your trailer. I get how angry you are."

"You don't know shit, bitch." Two more shots fired in her direction.

"Oh God, Dad, please hang on."

She peeked up over the plywood, saw David putting pressure on his dad's chest and crying. If Doyle Benson was still alive, he wouldn't be for long unless she did something soon.

"Come on, Jeb," she called out. "We know about your mom. About the life you got stuck with. It sucks, I know it does. I had a suck-ass childhood, too. I can help you. I can make them understand you need help, not jail."

Her kind offer was met with more foul words and another shot. Seven shots total, if she wasn't mistaken. She hadn't heard him reload, and she wondered what make of gun he had.

"Jeb, trust me—it's not worth hurting anyone else. Tell me what you need to make this better."

"Throw your gun down and come out, and I won't kill them both."

She peeked around the stack of plywood and saw Jeb with his gun aimed at David's head. The walls inside the condo were framed, but not dry-walled. She could see for quite a distance past Jeb. Ty was approaching Jeb's back like a panther.

"Okay. All right. Move your gun away from David's head and I'll throw down my gun and come out."

"Do it now, bitch."

Slowly she stood in full view and tossed her gun to the side to keep Jeb's focus away from Ty. Raising her hands in the air, she took a couple of steps to keep him centered on her movements.

"There's no sense in hurting David, Jeb. If you lose your brother, you'll regret it forever. Just give us a chance to help you."

Jeb squeezed off another round. The little shit nailed her in the upper arm. It stung like a son of a bitch.

Ty launched himself across the room and took Jeb down. A scuffle erupted and another shot rang out. A horrible sense of deja vu went through Jordan. Her heart reeled. Memories of Ty wrestling a drug runner to the ground on their last case flashed in her mind. She lunged forward and screamed his name.

Her world had hung in the balance that day, much like it did right now with some half-crazed punk wrapped around Ty's body.

But thank God, Ty moved, continuing to struggle with Jeb before clocking the troubled kid hard enough to knock him loopy.

Air rushed back into Jordan's lungs, but the edges of her vision darkened at the same time.

Ty had Jeb in handcuffs before she could think straight again.

When Ty stood, she pointed to David, who knelt in a puddle of blood and still cradled Doyle in his arms. Ty called for an ambulance and stripped off his sweatshirt and pushed it against Doyle's abdomen. "Keep firm pressure on that until help gets here," he said to David. Then he moved to Jordan and pointed to her arm. "Damn it, are you hit?"

"Not really," she said. "Just grazed my arm."

"Don't you ever listen?" He started searching her, moving his hands all over her body checking for injuries. "Don't do anything dangerous, Jordan. No heroics, Jordan. Promise me, Jordan."

"What about you?" she argued. "Did your academy teach you to jump on every dumb asshole with a gun in his hands? Law of averages says one of these times you're not going to get back up."

He got on his phone, spouted off something about another ambulance and officer down.

"I'm not down. I'm nowhere near down." She stood and turned in a circle just to prove her point. "See? I'll get checked out, but I'm not going in an ambulance. You know the media eats that shit up." She dropped back down on the stack of wood when the room spun.

Ty scooped her up, and she relaxed against his chest.

"Might as well be talking to a fucking brick wall. Damn it, woman, just once could you—"

"I love you." She smiled up at him. "And I can see it now. This is our picture—guns and dreams and bullets and bad guys."

His brows furrowed as he frowned down at her. "What are you saying, baby? Jesus, how much blood have you lost?"

She smiled. "Our picture. Our life together. The future. The one I could never see in my head," she rambled. Man, she was really, *really* tired. It was everything she could do to keep focused on his handsome face. "I can see it now. It doesn't have anything to do with houses, horses, or kids—you were right about that. Nothing else matters, it's just about us." She closed her eyes, thought she heard some rustling and movement that might have been the ambulance guys moving in. "Oh, and rockin' sex. It's because you're totally hung, but you and I have rockin' sex, don't we?"

"She, uh, has a bullet wound to the arm. She's lost some blood, apparently not thinking clearly at the moment." Ty's voice was all sexy and official-like as he spoke to the paramedics.

It made her giggle.

She wondered if maybe she should be embarrassed about something, but the feeling never really took hold. Being curled against Ty felt too damn good.

She closed her eyes, happy to be able to see the picture of her life with Ty. It wasn't normal. She wasn't normal. Their life together was never going to be normal, or glamorous, or a picture anyone else in the world could relate to, but it was their picture. And it was a pretty spectacular picture to drift off to.

The End

EPILOGUE

Ty decided *surly* was the best way to describe Jordan's mood. His mood wasn't much better. Luckily, the shot to her arm from Jeb Williams' gun was superficial. A few stitches and a sling and she was good to go, but the Dr. had ordered a week of bedrest. Jordan and bedrest mixed like oil and vinegar.

Three days in, and the damn woman was about to drive him out of his mind. He'd taken her on a short trip to the hospital to visit Doyle Benson. David's father had lost his spleen and undergone a lengthy surgery, but he was expected to fully recover. Unfortunately, David didn't appear to be doing quite as well.

"You could have at least taken me to Antonio's for pizza on the way home," she grumbled as they walked back into the house. "I told you I'm fine. I hate being under house arrest."

"It's not house arrest. The doctor said you were supposed to be on bedrest for a week. If you want pizza later, I'll go get pizza. Christ. I don't make the rules, I just follow them."

"Really," she shot back. "Since when?"

"Since you got a bullet hole put in your arm while helping with my case. Now damn it, you're supposed to be resting. Are we going to have this argument again?"

His irritation seemed to vaporize hers. She went to him, wrapped her good arm around his neck and kissed his cheek. "Please tell me you're not still twisted up because I got a little scratch on my arm helping you with a case. You know better than that. I'm a disaster magnet. Trouble follows me closer than my own shadow. What happened was not your fault."

"Really? Because if I hadn't dragged you along . . . " There was no point finishing the sentence. They both knew the truth. If he hadn't involved her, she wouldn't be injured right now.

She hooked a finger into his belt loop and pulled him in front of the couch. With a solid shove, she pushed him down, then crawled onto his lap. "Let me ask you something. Do you think you could ever stop being a cop? Because to me, it feels like once that's what you are, it's just in your blood. At any moment someone could take my badge, my gun, and my uniform. But no one will ever take my instincts, my curiosity, or my compulsive need to screw with people. So someone's always going to want to shoot me, and that's not your fault."

He smiled in spite of himself. "That may be true. Maybe neither of us will ever be fit to be anything but cops, but it doesn't change the fact that I hate you were shot helping with my case."

"Well, look on the bright side, maybe someday you can get shot helping with one of my cases if that makes you feel better," she teased. "More importantly, David and Doyle Benson are alive and they're going to be fine. We did a good thing together."

He grinned. "A lot of what we do together is good."

"Really, *really* good," she agreed.

He pulled her head closer and kissed her temple. "You think David will bounce back from this? I could hardly stand to look at him today. He seemed so . . . torn up."

Beauty wiggled and groaned and laid her muzzle on Ty's knee.

Jordan reached out and scratched the dog's ears. "I think in time he'll come around," she finally said. "He's a good kid. He's had a good life, so hopefully with his dad's support, he'll come through it. Still, he lost the love of his life, almost watched his dad die. And on top of it, it was his own brother that wanted to kill him. That's not a good week by anyone's standard."

"I know, right? So by comparison, spending a week lounging on the couch and being catered to by me shouldn't be that bad." Ty nudged Beauty to the side and turned Jordan until she straddled his lap. "You think you'll survive it?"

She rolled her eyes and blew out an exaggerated sigh. "Maybe. But you're going to have to work awfully hard at entertaining me."

"Yeah?" He thrust his hips up just to tease her. "What did you have in mind?"

She kissed a hot streak up his neck, sucked his earlobe between her teeth, and then whispered, "Antonio's pizza."

A couple of hours later, Ty had everything under control. Except his heartrate. And his hands were sweaty. He wiped them on his jeans and entered the house through the kitchen door.

Jordan was sitting on the couch reading a magazine. She didn't bother to look up when he entered. "Cowboy, as far as keeping me entertained, you suck. Where have you been?"

"Antonio's. My lady wanted pizza, so we're going to have pizza. I just popped it in the oven to keep in warm." Trying desperately to pull off calm and casual, he sat on the coffee table in front of her. "I've been thinking about what you said. I guess it would drive me crazy to be cooped up in here, too. I don't think it will hurt for you to get some fresh air before we eat."

She tossed the magazine and met his gaze. "Really? Where are we going?" She popped up off the couch. "Actually, I don't even care as long as I get out of the house. I'm going to get my shoes."

"Why don't you get your boots?" he said, halting her in her tracks. "It's a pretty night. Lots of stars. I know how much you like it out by the pond. I thought maybe we could take a walk out there and sit on the swing, get a little fresh air. Then we'll come back and eat."

At first, she narrowed her eyes as if she were going to question him, but then she apparently decided not to. She shrugged. "Okay."

Thank God she didn't push for details. His nerves were fraying a little more with each minute that went by. He took a deep breath and let it out slowly, praying he was doing the right thing. Nothing like a gunshot to get you thinking about your future. Particularly after the doctor pointed out that if Jordan's wound had been a few inches to the left, the results would have been much different.

"I'm good to go." Jordan hopped off the last step like a kid going to the fair. "Except I need you to zip my coat over this stupid sling. And I can't find Beauty's leash, but she'll stay with us if we're just going to the pond." Finally, she took a breath and looked at him. "What?"

He grinned and shook his head. "Nothing."

"Nothing as in your completely annoyed with me? Or nothing as in you can't wait to have sex later? See, I need to know because I might have to go put on a prettier bra."

He stepped close and zipped her jacket. "Like an ugly bra would ever stop me."

She giggled. "True. You tend to be the black knight of death as far as my bras go. I'm not sure why I even bother."

"Hey, braless works for me," he said tugging her toward the back door. Beauty pranced out in front of them. "You want to walk or ride the four-wheeler to the pond."

"Walk, if it's okay with you."

Ty stuck a flashlight in his pocket and locked up the house. They held hands in silence for most of the way. At the end of the trail, Jordan stopped and turned to him. "I hope you're not mad at me. I'm sorry I've been a bitch, but I don't need to be under house arrest because of a couple stitches in my arm."

He put his hands on her hips and pulled her close. "You're probably right. But being able to keep track of you for a day or so sure made me feel better." Softly, he touched his lips to hers. She wrapped her good arm around his neck and coaxed that short kiss into a long, greedy tangle of emotion.

When they came up for air, he took her hand and led her to the swing at the edge of the pond. They sat and swayed in the cool night air. Ty tried like hell to think of something clever to say, but this was harder than he thought. Everything he came up with sounded idiotic.

"You're very quiet tonight. I could be wrong, but I'm sensing something is going on. Something more than my bad attitude." She put a finger on his chin and urged him to look at her. "Talk to me."

She was right. He needed to pull it together. It was now or never. He stopped the swing and shifted toward her. "Whenever you get hurt, it reminds me of what we do for a living. Reminds me we don't wake up and sit at a nice, safe desk job all day. We don't teach kids or sell real estate. We work with criminals. Sometimes I worry that, you know, something could happen to one of us."

She was quiet for a long moment. "I know. I worry about that, too. But people die in car accidents every day going to their nice, safe desk jobs. You can't predict the future, Ty. And maybe sometimes our jobs get a little dangerous, but cop work is also exciting and every day is different. That's what I love about it. Would you want to sit at a desk? Hell, Ty, I couldn't even stand to stay inside the house for a week."

He grinned. "A fact I'm well aware of."

"You say that like it's a bad thing." She poked his arm. "Come on, you don't want me to quit my job do you?"

"No. That's not at all what I was getting at."

"Okay. Then what *are* you getting at?"

Ty stood and turned toward her. "Jesus, this is terrifying." He took her hand in his but then quickly dropped it. "Oh shit. I forgot something." He jogged to the edge of the tree line where Trevor had installed the electrical system and flipped a switch.

The trees around the lake lit up like a drive-through Christmas park. The sight of it was fairly spectacular if he did say so himself. Many of the lights twinkled and the beautiful reflection off of the pond was almost breathtaking. It was hard to believe they pulled it off.

He jogged back to Jordan who was now standing with her mouth hanging open.

"Oh my God," she said, no small amount of wonder in her voice. "When did you have time to do this?"

When he dropped to one knee and pulled out a ring box she actually squealed and started to cry. It may have been the most genuinely female thing he'd ever seen her do.

He took her hand and squeezed it. "Jordan Delany. I've never loved someone the way I love you. Sometimes I don't even think what I feel is normal or rational. I don't want to waste any more time, or take any more chances that something will happen to one of us before you become Mrs. Tyler McGee. I love you, Jordan Delany. Will you marry me?"

ABOUT THE AUTHOR

Award-winning author, Michelle Sharp, has been nominated for a 2014 National Readers Choice Award for Best Romantic Suspense and Best First Book. In addition, her debut novel Dream Huntress has been selected as a finalist in the 2015 Daphne Du Maurier award for Excellence in Mystery and Suspense. Although she has a degree in Journalism from Southern Illinois University, she finds weaving tales of danger, deception, and love much preferable to reporting the cold, hard facts. Her goal in life? To team resilient, kickass heroines with the sexy Alpha's who love them.

As most authors probably are, she is an avid reader. Her family may even call it obsessive. Growing up in St. Louis has made her a die-hard Cardinals fan, and having a child with Down Syndrome has made her passionate about any issue regarding special needs kiddos. She's also a fairly big sucker when it comes to anything with fur or feathers.

Michelle is a proud member of Romance Writers of America and Missouri Romance Writers. You can learn more about her at michelleshapbooks.com, where you will also find links to her social media.

Made in the USA
San Bernardino, CA
25 October 2015